Chicken Mission

The Curse of Fogsham Farm

Jennifer Gray lives in London and Scotland with her husband, four children and friendly but enigmatic cat, Henry. Her other work includes the Atticus Claw series and the Guinea Pigs Online books, co-written with Amanda Swift. The first book in the Atticus series, *Atticus Claw Breaks the Law*, was shortlisted for the Waterstones Children's Book Prize and won the 2014 Red House Children's Book Award – Younger Readers category.

BY THE SAME AUTHOR

Atticus Claw Breaks the Law
Atticus Claw Settles a Score
Atticus Claw Lends a Paw
Atticus Claw Goes Ashore
Atticus Claw Learns to Draw
Chicken Mission: Danger in the Deep Dark Woods

Chicken Mission

The Curse of Fogsham Farm

JENNIFER GRAY

ff

First published in 2015
by Faber & Faber Limited
Bloomsbury House, 74–77 Great Russell Street,
London WC1B 3DA

Typeset by Crow Books
Printed in the UK by CPI Group (UK) Ltd, Croydon, CR0 4YY

A CIP record for this book
is available from the British Library

ISBN 978–0–571–29829–7

2 4 6 8 10 9 7 5 3 1

To Amanda
with special thanks to Keren, Lydia, Becky,
Anna and Fenella

Prologue

High on the windswept moor lies a farmhouse. It occupies a desolate spot, surrounded by stark heather-covered hills as far as the eye can see. The farmhouse belongs to two elderly humans, who open it in the summer as a bed and breakfast for passing tourists. In the winter the humans hole themselves up in the farmhouse against the cold and the farmyard is bleak and empty. The sheep are left to roam the moor. The cows are tucked up snugly in the barn. And, apart from a generous daily ration of grain delivered by the humans each morning at dawn to their sheds, the chickens of Fogsham Farm are left to their own devices.

On this particular evening in the depths of a biting January, Ichabod Comb, a muscular but battle-scarred rooster, was closing up one of the chicken sheds for the night. The shed went by the name of The Bloodless Hen amongst the chickens of Fogsham

1

Farm. The Bloodless Hen was a chicken-style juice-bar where they all congregated in the evenings to chat over a worm juice and a bag of grub scratchings. It was Ichabod Comb's job to look after the place. Ichabod yawned. It was past nine o'clock and he was tired. It had been a busy evening what with the quiz and no one else behind the bar to help him. He glanced at the mess. The upturned wooden crates, which served as tables, were strewn with plastic cups, not to mention screwed-up bits of paper and crayon butts. Ichabod Comb cursed softly.

'See you later, Ichabod,' the last chicken said as the others straggled out. 'We'll leave the door of the sleeping coop unlatched for you.' The chickens usually slept together in another one of the sheds to keep warm.

Ichabod Comb shook his head. 'I think I'll just stay here tonight, Rossiter, and get the clearing up done,' he said. 'I've got to be up early in the morning to start crowing, otherwise the humans will be late with the grain.'

'Are you sure?' his friend asked.

'Yes,' Ichabod Comb said firmly. 'Thanks anyway.'

Rossiter Brown hesitated. 'Well, watch how you go, Ichabod,' he said eventually. 'We'll see you tomorrow.' He scuttled off across the farmyard after the others.

Ichabod Comb peered after him into the mist. He shivered. Fogsham Farm was creepy in winter. There were five chicken sheds in total: the juice shed, the shop, the school, the leisure centre and the cosy sleeping coop where the chickens went at night to roost and lay the occasional egg. The sheds were next to the barn, where the cows were kept. Behind them was the dry stone wall that ran round the perimeter of the farmyard. Beyond that a footpath led across the hillside to a ruined stone church, and from there to Bloodsucker Hall.

Bloodsucker Hall was tucked away behind crumbling brick walls and rusty spiked gates in the lee of the hill. You could barely see it from the farmyard, even on a nice day. And, as far as Ichabod Comb was concerned, you didn't want to.

He had been to Bloodsucker Hall once: just once

– when he first arrived and heard about the curse of Fogsham Farm. The farm chickens had been eager to fill him in on the legend surrounding the hall's last occupant – a ferocious mink known as Countess Stella von Fangula. They told him how the mink sucked the blood of her victims; how she had become a vampire; how she had been sent to her grave by a pheasants' revolt; and how she had sworn that she would rise again if she ever caught the whiff of fresh rooster blood in her nostrils . . .

Ichabod Comb wasn't a bird who spooked easily. He'd been in some tough spots in his life – including a tour of Afghanistan with the Yorkshire Rooster Regiment. He wasn't afraid of some stupid legend about a vampire mink. On his next day off he had climbed through a hole in the dry stone wall and taken the path across the moor to check the place out. He had ducked through the rusty gates of the hall and scuttled through the abandoned garden. It was when he was climbing the dilapidated steps to the front door that he had trodden on a broken slate which had fallen from the crumbling roof.

 4

He had felt a sharp pain in his foot and glanced down to see a drop of blood oozing from a cut. The rooster's courage had failed him. What if the curse was true? What if the Countess von Fangula really was a vampire? What if she smelled his blood and rose from her grave? Ichabod Comb had raced away from the hall. Ignoring the pain in his foot he had dodged through the jungle of bushes back to the path across the moor. He had hurried past the ruined church, squeezed through the hole in the dry stone wall and scuttled back across the farmyard to the sleeping coop to join his friends.

Ichabod Comb never returned to Bloodsucker Hall. He stayed at the chicken sheds. Mostly he went from the sleeping coop to the juice shed and back again. Occasionally he visited the shop. On his days off he went to the leisure centre with Rossiter, but he never did any exercise because of his injured foot.

Gradually, the memory of Bloodsucker Hall faded.

But sometimes, like tonight, the fear returned.

Telling himself not to be so silly, Ichabod Comb stepped back inside the juice shed and closed the door firmly behind him.

It was then that he saw that one customer still remained – a hunched figure in the corner wearing a black hooded cloak. It didn't look like any of his regulars. Perhaps it was one of the pheasants from the moor.

'We're closed,' he said.

'*Reaalllly*, darling?' The stranger was female. She had a low, sultry voice. 'That's a shame.'

Ichabod Comb couldn't place the voice. It was pleasant, rich and melodic, like beautiful music. For some reason it made him feel drowsy.

'Can't I just have one little drink?' the cloaked figure whispered. 'It's such a cold night. And there's no heating in the house.'

'You should get that fixed,' the innkeeper suggested.

'Yes, darling, I should,' the stranger agreed. 'And the roof. The slates keep falling off.' She sighed. 'Such a nuisance! It's just that I've been away for a long time. I haven't got round to it yet.'

Ichabod Comb yawned. He could barely keep his eyes open. 'All right,' he said sleepily. 'I'll get you a drink. What would you like?'

'A Bloody Mary.' The cloaked figure got up and slunk towards the bar. 'Make it nice and bloody.'

Ichabod Comb looked about for a clean cup. There were none: the chickens had used them all up. He reached instead for the single china thimble that sat on the shelf behind the bar. One of the chickens had found it in the rubbish. Ichabod Comb didn't usually use it because it had a small chip in it: you could cut yourself if you weren't careful.

Clumsily he poured a shot of worm juice into the thimble and mixed it with a squashed tomato. He felt as if he were in a trance. 'Here you are.' He went to place the thimble on the bar but he missed. The thimble dropped onto the wooden floor of the chicken shed and shattered at his feet.

'Sorry,' he mumbled. The innkeeper bent down and started to pick up the pieces of china. 'Ouch!' One of the sharp shards cut his wing. A drop of blood glistened on his feathers. He stood up groggily and felt for a tea towel to dab it with.

'How clever of you, darling!' The hooded figure had reached the bar. She leaned towards him, the

cloak still wrapped closely around her.

'Clever?' Ichabod Comb repeated thickly. 'What do you mean?'

'To know that I prefer *real* blood, darling!' The stranger laughed. 'But of course you remember that from the time you visited me at Bloodsucker Hall and woke me up, don't you?'

A paw shot out from under the cloak and gripped Ichabod Comb by the neck. The stranger drew the terrified bird towards her. She took a deep, satisfied sniff. 'Rooster blood,' she breathed. 'About time.'

Chapter One

At Chicken HQ, Amy Cluckbucket sat on a garden stool playing *Chicken World Wrestling 3* on the laptop. Wrestling was Amy's number one favourite sport. She was actually pretty good at it herself.

Pictures of the competitors lined up on the screen. They were all based on real-life chicken wrestling champions. Amy chose one and clicked on the mouse.

'Rocky Terminegger!' the computer confirmed her selection.

Amy had a massive crush on Rocky Terminegger. Her greatest wish was to meet him one day and get his clawtograph. She waited to see who Rocky's opponent would be.

'Granny Wishbone!' shouted the computer.

Amy groaned. Granny Wishbone was the dirtiest fighter in the game and a dreadful cheat. She somersaulted into the ring with her Zimmer frame.

Amy watched her shrewdly.

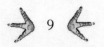

The Zimmer frame was similar to a four-legged stool without the seat; the idea being that Granny Wishbone could lean on it if she needed to because she was very old. In fact, as Amy well knew, Granny Wishbone just used it to bash the other wrestlers with when the referee wasn't looking.

The bell sounded. 'Round one!' said the referee.

Amy tapped at the keys.

KAPOW! Rocky threw Granny Wishbone over his shoulder.

WHACK! Granny Wishbone fought back with her Zimmer frame.

THONK! Rocky got her in a headlock.

CLATTER! Granny Wishbone's teeth fell out.

PUNCH! Granny Wishbone pinned Rocky with her Zimmer frame and elbowed him sharply in the neck.

'Fowl!' Amy protested.

'End of round one,' the referee yelled.

'Phew!' Amy stretched her wings. 'That old bird puts up a peck of a fight. Does anyone else want a go?' she called. (She didn't really want to give anyone else a turn but when she lived at Perrin's Farm with her parents, her mother had told her it was polite to ask.)

'No thanks, Amy,' said Ruth. Her voice sounded muffled. 'I've got to change the tube on the mite blaster.'

Amy glanced up. Chicken HQ consisted of three potting sheds, each with its own green door, which had all been joined together inside to make a huge space. The laptop was in the middle on an upturned crate. At one end was a cupboard full of cool chicken gadgets. It was from here that Ruth's voice came.

'Then I'm going to work on my latest invention.' Ruth emerged from the cupboard with the mite blaster. She was a white chicken with looping black tail feathers, a grey scarf and spectacles, which kept falling down. She pushed them back up her beak and started to unscrew the tube carefully.

'What *is* your latest invention?' Amy enquired.

'I don't know, I haven't invented it yet,' Ruth said.

'What about you, Boo?' Amy asked. 'Do you want a turn?'

'Maybe later,' Boo said, 'after my bath.' From the other end of the sheds came the sound of running water.

Amy turned her head towards the chickens' sleeping quarters. Each chicken had a straw pallet that folded up into the wall at the press of a button. Beside their beds stood a birdbath with a hosepipe which fed into it from the garden tap.

Boo held up a packet of Bird Bright and read the instructions out loud.

'Add one measure to make your feathers shine! Two to make them sparkle!'

Boo tipped in three measures. 'Shall I save the water for you?' she asked Amy. Boo was a beautiful chicken with glossy, honey-coloured feathers and gorgeous feathery boots, which she was very proud of. She was also brilliant at gymnastics.

'Er, no thanks,' Amy said quickly. She wasn't very keen on baths; at least not ones that involved water. She preferred to rub her feathers in dust.

'Okay,' said Boo. 'Give me a shout if you change your mind.' She climbed into the bubbles.

Amy got up from her stool with a deep sigh of satisfaction. She loved being part of an elite chicken combat squat. Boo and Ruth were her best friends. And Chicken HQ was a really cool place to live. Their boss, Professor Rooster, had thought of everything. The only problem was that, since they had defeated Thaddeus E. Fox and his MOST WANTED Club of villains, things at Chicken HQ had been a bit quiet. Amy couldn't wait for their next mission.

She bustled over to the mini-fridge to get an apple core. Amy was shorter than the other two chickens. She had to stand on her tiptoes to reach the shelf. In fact, Amy wasn't just short, she was small all over except for her tummy, which had puffs of dark and light grey feathers around it and made her look plump. She also had very red cheeks, which glowed when she was excited or cross.

'Time for round two.' Amy finished the apple core and returned to the laptop.

Just then the screen fizzed into life. Amy felt a little shiver of excitement.

'It's Professor Rooster!' she cried.

 14

'Maybe he's got another mission for us!' exclaimed Ruth. She put down the mite blaster.

'Wait for me!' Boo shook her gleaming feathers dry and raced over.

The three chickens crowded round the laptop.

A very stern-looking cockerel appeared on the screen. His face was grave.

'Looks like it's something serious,' Ruth whispered.

'You don't think Thaddeus E. Fox and his MOST WANTED Club are back, do you?' Boo hissed.

Amy didn't say anything. She was too excited to speak.

'It's not Fox,' Professor Rooster said shortly. (It was a two-way monitor so the professor could see and hear the chickens as well.) 'It's worse.'

Worse?! Amy blinked. What could be worse than Thaddeus E. Fox and his gang?

Professor Rooster looked straight at them. 'Chickens,' he said, 'we've got a vampire problem.'

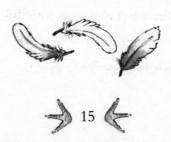

Chapter Two

There was a shocked silence. Amy wished Boo or Ruth would say something, but they didn't. Eventually she picked up the courage to speak. She gave a nervous giggle. 'A vampire problem!' she echoed. 'Are you joking, Professor?'

'No, Amy, I am not joking,' Professor Rooster said sharply. 'I never joke when chickens' lives are at stake. You should know that by now.'

'Sorry,' Amy mumbled. She felt silly. For a moment she'd forgotten that Thaddeus E. Fox had been responsible for the deaths of Professor Rooster's wife and chicks. That's why the professor had brought Boo, Ruth and Amy together – to protect other chickens from evil predators.

'It's time to introduce you to the most MOST WANTED criminal known to chickens,' Professor Rooster continued grimly.

'But I thought that was Thaddeus E. Fox!' Amy squawked.

'So did I,' Professor Rooster said, 'until I heard about the curse of Fogsham Farm.'

Amy gulped. *A curse?* She didn't like the sound of that one little bit.

'Where's Fogsham Farm?' Ruth had found her voice.

'Fogsham Farm is situated in the small hamlet of Bleakley Fogsham,' said the professor. 'It's about twenty miles away from here as the crow flies . . .' he paused. '. . . on the moor.'

The moor! Amy had heard of the moor but the chickens had never been there. Chicken HQ was in the grounds of Dudley Manor, in the old walled vegetable garden. Dudley Manor itself was a grand park with a big stately home in the middle of it, with a river and green fields to one side and the Deep Dark Woods, where Thaddeus E. Fox had his burrow, to the other. The moor was somewhere to the north. Amy knew little about it, except it wasn't the sort of place a chicken would go to, especially in January.

'As you can see, it's a desolate spot,' Professor Rooster said.

A gloomy picture of a stone farmhouse flashed up on the screen. Next to it stood a barn and five chicken sheds. The buildings were surrounded by a dry stone wall. That was it. Amy felt sorry for the chickens of Fogsham Farm; it looked like a miserable place to live.

'Apart from the farm, there's a ruined church . . .' the professor paused, '. . . beyond that is Bloodsucker Hall.'

The next picture was of a huge building tucked away behind crumbling brick walls and rusty spiked metal gates.

Amy shivered. The house looked seriously spooky.

'Two hundred years ago Bloodsucker Hall was home to a notorious predator: a mink named Countess Stella von Fangula,' the professor continued. 'She spread terror amongst the birds of the moor, including the chickens of Fogsham Farm. Her favourite drink was rooster blood.'

Amy blinked. *Rooster blood!* This was getting really freaky.

'Let me tell you something about mink,' Professor Rooster said. 'A mink is an animal that can climb trees and swim to depths of thirty metres. It can run as fast as a deer and squeeze unseen through tiny gaps, like a spider. It has razor sharp claws and fangs like a crocodile. It can kill any bird with one swipe of its paw. Worst of all, it has a lust for blood. It will murder every bird it sees . . . but it won't eat it. All a mink wants to do is to suck the blood of its poultry prey,' he paused, 'like a vampire.'

Ruth put her wing up. 'But minks aren't really vampires, Professor,' she reasoned. 'They're just animals.'

'You're right, Ruth, of course,' Professor Rooster acknowledged. 'As a general rule, minks are not true vampires even thought they behave like them.' He allowed himself a grim smile. 'Fortunately for us chickens, they do not usually live forever.'

Amy felt relieved. She had almost thought Professor Rooster was talking about a real vampire for a minute!

'HOWEVER,' the professor went on in a voice that made Amy's heart sink, 'it seems that the Countess Stella von Fangula may be an exception to the general rule.' He waved a yellowing book at the camera. 'According to this, the countess loved the taste of bird blood so much she concocted a potion to give her eternal life.' Professor Rooster adjusted his specs and began to read.

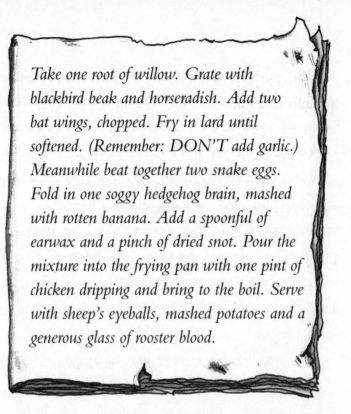

Take one root of willow. Grate with blackbird beak and horseradish. Add two bat wings, chopped. Fry in lard until softened. (Remember: DON'T add garlic.) Meanwhile beat together two snake eggs. Fold in one soggy hedgehog brain, mashed with rotten banana. Add a spoonful of earwax and a pinch of dried snot. Pour the mixture into the frying pan with one pint of chicken dripping and bring to the boil. Serve with sheep's eyeballs, mashed potatoes and a generous glass of rooster blood.

'*Eerrrggghhh!*' Amy put her wing over her mouth. 'Someone pass the sick bucket.'

Professor Rooster ignored her. 'It seems that the potion worked. Fangula became an actual vampire, feeding off innocent birds as before, only this time there was a difference.'

'Did they turn into vampires too?' Amy asked in an awed voice.

'Not quite, Amy,' Professor Rooster said. 'When a vampire mink sucks the blood of another creature it becomes a zombie. Very soon Fangula had an army of zombie poultry at her command.'

Amy risked another glance at Boo. Boo's face was still frozen in a petrified expression.

'Eventually, after many years, the local pheasant population revolted,' the professor continued. 'They marched on Bloodsucker Hall in the dead of night, slipped through the gate and flocked up the steps to meet Fangula's zombie army.'

Professor Rooster raised the book again.

The zombie army was dreadful in its look, with drooling beaks and staring eyes. It swept towards the brave pheasants through the fog with the countess at the fore. Her fangs were bared, ready to bite the heads clean off her enemies, which she did with much joy and gnashing. The pheasants scattered in all directions, save one young bird, stouter of spirit than the rest. He stepped forward with a wooden pencil in his wing, sharpened to a point, and threw it at the countess. It struck her in the chest and pierced her heart.

'I will return!' she shrieked. 'At the first sniff of rooster blood, I will rise again and take my revenge upon the birds of Bleakley Fogsham.'

And with that she fell to the ground dead. The zombie army, seeing this, disappeared into the mist.'

Amy stared wide-eyed at the professor. 'What happened next?' she whispered.

'The countess was buried in the grounds of Bloodsucker Hall in an iron coffin,' Professor Rooster said. 'Everyone thought she'd gone for good. Until Ichabod Comb, the landlord of The Bloodless Hen juice shed disappeared last night.'

The Bloodless Hen juice shed? Amy gulped. This was getting freakier and freakier. 'But how do you know the countess took him?' she asked. 'Maybe it was a fox.'

'There are no foxes on the moor in winter,' Professor Rooster replied crisply. 'They go to ground. Besides, Ichabod Comb confided in one of his friends at the farm: a rooster called Rossiter Brown. Ichabod told Rossiter he went snooping up at the hall a few weeks ago and cut his foot on a broken roof slate.' He stopped to let his words sink in.

Ruth was the first to understand. 'If the curse is true, the countess would have smelled his rooster blood and risen from the grave!' she whispered.

'Eggsactly,' Professor Rooster agreed. 'Ichabod Comb woke her up when he cut his foot. That's why she chose him as her first victim. All that was found at the juice shed this morning by the other chickens was a broken thimble and a trail of blood leading in the direction of Bloodsucker Hall.'

Suddenly Boo let out a terrified squawk. 'You mean Ichabod Comb is a zombie?' she screeched.

Amy tried hard to imagine what a zombie chicken might look like and what she'd do if she ever saw one. She didn't think wrestling them would work: their wings would probably fall off.

'I fear so, chickens,' Professor Rooster said gravely. 'And a very dangerous one at that. He's young, strong and fit. His blood will keep Fangula going for a while. After that she'll want more. Any of the chickens at Fogsham Farm could be her next victim, although she'd prefer rooster if she can get it. You have to stop her. Before she strikes again. The obvious target is the farm. But she's a mink. She can travel long distances.' He paused. 'We are *all* in danger, including the chickens of Dudley Manor Coop.'

'But how *can* we stop her, Professor?' Boo wailed. 'She might turn *us* into zombies!'

'We could use the mite blaster,' Ruth suggested. 'We could put garlic in it instead of mites. Vampires hate garlic.'

'It might hold her for a bit,' Professor Rooster said, 'especially if you crush the garlic first. But it won't stop her for long.' He fixed them with his sternest look.

Amy had a bad feeling about what was coming next.

'The best way to kill a vampire mink is the same way the pheasants did it in 1887,' the professor told

them, 'with a wooden stake through her heart.' The monitor began to fizzle. 'You'll need a pencil, a sharpener and a hammer. You'll find all three in the Emergency Chicken Pack. Good luck.'

Chapter Three

The three chickens sat around the laptop, arguing.

'I can't,' Boo said.

'Neither can I.' Amy pulled a face.

'Well, don't look at me,' Ruth said. 'I'm not doing it.'

'One of us has to finish her off,' Amy argued back.

'But you heard what the professor said,' Boo sniffed. 'The best way to get rid of Fangula is with a stake through her heart.'

'And I can't stand the sight of blood,' Ruth said.

'Neither can I!' Boo wailed. 'Are you sure you can't do it, Amy?' she pleaded. 'I mean, it's more your sort of thing than mine and Ruth's.'

Amy knew what Boo was getting at. The chickens had been selected to join Professor Rooster's elite combat squad because they each had a special skill. Ruth's was intelligence; Boo's was perseverance; and Amy's was courage, which was why the other two expected *her* to do it. Her cheeks felt very red and hot. In spite of herself she was cross with Professor Rooster. It was the first time anyone had mentioned slaying vampire minks as part of their job description. She ignored Boo's question. 'Why doesn't the professor do it?' she grumbled. 'I mean, it's roosters Fangula likes best. It seems more fitting, somehow.'

Ruth sighed. 'Professor Rooster's the boss. It's not his job to do it. That's why he recruited us: to save chickens from evil predators. We're the trained warriors. Maybe if we all work together it will be okay. We'll just have to think of a plan.'

'Yeah, like getting someone else to do it,' Amy said stubbornly.

Just then there was a knock at one of the doors.

'I'll go,' Amy said gloomily. She jumped down off the garden stool.

'Hang on a minute,' Ruth said. 'No one knows we're here except the professor and he never visits.'

Professor Rooster was obsessed with secrecy. No one else was allowed to know the location of

Chicken HQ, and even the chickens didn't know where Professor Rooster's hideout was.

'Maybe it's the MOST WANTED Club!' Boo hissed. 'Maybe they're back! Maybe they've blown our cover.'

Amy backed away. Then she panicked: she'd had another idea. 'Maybe it's the Countess Stella von Fangula, come to suck our blood!' she squawked. 'Quick! Ruth, get the mite blaster!'

Ruth hurried off.

'Boo, go and see if we've got any garlic!' Amy ordered.

'There isn't time!' Boo flapped about in panic.

'I can't find the tube!' Ruth shouted from the cupboard. 'I put it down somewhere . . .'

The knocking came again – louder this time.

'It's too late!' Amy cried. 'Quick! Hide!'

The chickens burrowed into their straw beds.

CRASH!

The door flew open. Amy peeped through the stalks of hay. A large mallard stepped into the potting sheds. He was wearing a bow tie.

'Oh, no,' Amy groaned. 'It's James Pond. I'd rather it was Thaddeus E. Fox than that bossy big-head!'

James Pond was a duck agent who worked for Poultry Patrol. Professor Rooster had drafted him in to help the chickens once before, although as things turned out they had successfully completed their first mission without him.

The chickens came out from their hiding places.

'The name's Pond,' James Pond said smoothly. 'James Pond.'

'We know!' Amy said crossly. 'We've already met you, remember?'

'All right, keep your feathers on,' James Pond retorted. 'I just came to check if you hens needed help.'

Amy felt her cheeks glow red again. *I just came to check if you hens needed help!* Who did he think he was! Last time James Pond was supposed to help them, he'd been tricked into flying south early for the winter by Thaddeus E. Fox. Not that they'd needed help in the first place, of course! 'We're managing fine, thanks!' she fumed. 'Why are you even here, anyway? It's winter. You hate the winter.'

'Poultry Patrol got in touch,' James Pond explained. 'They begged me to return. I couldn't refuse.'

'Good for you,' Amy said sarcastically. 'Have fun!' She held the door open.

James Pond didn't budge. 'Are you quite *sure* you hens don't need help?' He glanced at Amy's tummy. 'Looks like you could use some keep fit training,' he remarked, giving it a prod. 'Tell you what,' he offered, 'I could stand on your feet while you do fifty sit-ups.'

'It's just feathers,' Amy said firmly, 'and no thanks.'

James Pond had put them through some keep fit training once before and she didn't intend to repeat the experience.

'Well, good luck with your next mission.' James Pond finally made to leave.

Their next mission . . . Amy blinked. *Wait a minute* . . . She frowned, her little brain had just registered the germ of an idea. She wrestled with it mentally for a few seconds. Then she grinned. *Bingo!* Amy felt very pleased with herself: she had just had one of her very occasional strokes of chicken genius! 'On

second thoughts,' she said, closing the door hastily, 'why don't you stay for a little while? That is, if you're not in a rush to get somewhere.'

'Huh?' Boo and Ruth looked at Amy in astonishment.

Amy gave them each a nudge. 'Fangula!' she mouthed. 'We can get Pond to do it!' She made a punching motion with her wing against her chest, then keeled over.

Boo's face lit up. So did Ruth's. The two chickens nodded their understanding.

'Yes, *do* tell us about your holiday,' Boo said politely. She ushered James Pond to one of the garden stools.

'How *was* your time in the Caribbean?' Ruth asked. 'I'd love to know.'

'Busy,' James Pond boasted, easing his backside onto the stool. 'If I wasn't dive-bombing rodents I was outsmarting stray cats! And if I wasn't outsmarting stray cats, I was dismantling bird booby traps with my beak. Still, I nailed the villains and saved the world's migrating birds, so I guess it was worth it.' He yawned. 'And that was just on the first morning!'

'Wow!' said Boo. 'That's impressive!' She gave Amy a wink.

'Thanks,' James Pond got up. 'Well, I guess if there really is nothing you hens need help with, I'll get going.'

'Actually,' Amy said, pushing him back down again, 'there *is* something . . .' Her voice trailed off.

'Oh yeah?' James Pond looked interested. 'Want me to dive-bomb some bad guys for you?'

'Not so much dive-bomb . . .' Ruth began. She looked at Amy.

'It's way more fun than that!' Amy assured him. 'Much more of a *challenge*. You'll love it, honest.'

'More fun than dive-bombing?' James Pond smirked. 'What, you mean like booting them in the backside with my enormous feet?'

Amy winked at the others. 'I'd say it's even better than that, wouldn't you?'

'Way better,' Ruth and Boo agreed.

James Pond looked intrigued. 'Wait! Will I get my

feathers dirty?' he asked suspiciously.

'Not necessarily,' Ruth said seriously. 'But it would probably be better to wear waterproof overalls and a pair of rubber boots just in case.'

Amy pulled a face then twisted it quickly into a smile so that James Pond wouldn't notice.

'So what's the job?' James Pond demanded.

'Vampire slaying,' Amy explained casually, as if it was just the sort of thing they did every day. 'The Countess Stella von Fangula has risen from her grave in the hamlet of Bleakley Fogsham. It's on the moor apparently. She's a vampire mink, you know – a real one. And the professor needs someone to drive a stake through her heart. I mean, we'd love to do it . . .'

'But we think you'd be better at it,' Ruth gushed.

'Cos you're so cool,' Boo finished.

The chickens held their breath.

'All right.' James Pond agreed. 'I guess I could spare a couple of days.' He reached under his wing and drew out a slim leather case from a holster. 'It's lucky for you I picked up a new one of these last time

I was in Transylvania. That place is full of vampires.'
He handed the case to Amy.

Amy opened it carefully. It contained a slim plastic
cylinder, a pencil, a sharpener and a plastic handle
with a trigger.

'Don't you need a hammer?' Ruth asked.

'Nope, not with this baby.' James Pond looked smug.

Amy passed the instructions to Ruth. (Amy wasn't
very good at reading.)

Ruth read them out loud.

VLADIMIR'S VAMPIRE SLAYER

*Instructions: Open vampire's coffin. Screw
tube onto handle. Secure sharpened pencil
in tube with sharp end pointing towards
vampire. Position yourself directly above
coffin. Taking care that vampire does not
wake up, take aim and fire.*

*For Best Results: ensure pencil penetrates
vampire's heart.*

*CAUTION: Contains small parts. Do
not place in the way of baby chicks.*

'Gosh,' she said. 'I wish I'd invented something as
clever as that!'

'You will, Ruth, don't worry,' Amy told her. She
examined the packet. 'Have you used it before?' she
asked James Pond.

The duck appeared astonished at the question.

'Sure I have. I've slain more vampires than you've laid eggs.'

Amy looked dubious. She hadn't laid *any* eggs yet, although she hoped she might start soon. Then again, James Pond seemed to know what he was talking about.

'The trick is to catch them during the day when they're asleep,' James Pond said. 'They never go out in daylight or they get fried.' He replaced the leather case in the holster. 'Shall we?' He nodded towards the door.

'Okay,' Amy agreed. 'Give us a minute.'

The chickens rushed about collecting their equipment. Ruth ticked off a list.

'Flight-booster engines?'

'Check,' said Amy.

'Super-spec headsets?'

'Check,' said Boo.

'Mite blaster?'

'Check.'

'Spare garlic tubes?'

'Check.'

'Emergency Chicken Pack?'

'What's the point of that?' Amy asked. 'We won't need it now.'

'We should probably take it just in case,' Ruth said. She threw it into her backpack.

The three chickens strapped on their flight-booster engines.

'Wait!' Boo said. 'Shouldn't we tell the professor?'

'Well . . .' Ruth hesitated.

They both looked at Amy.

'Nah,' said Amy. Telling the professor meant admitting that they needed help – from James Pond of all birds! 'The professor doesn't need to know,' she said. 'As long as we get the job done, who cares anyway?'

'I suppose so,' Boo said slowly. 'What do you think, Ruth?'

'I don't know . . .' Ruth frowned. 'Maybe we should . . .'

'Hurry up before I change my mind,' James Pond shouted.

'We don't have time to tell the professor!' Amy

squawked. 'If we don't go now we'll have to do it ourselves! And nobody wants that, do they?'

Boo and Ruth glanced at one another. Boo nodded. 'Okay,' Ruth agreed. 'I guess it won't hurt. We can always tell him when we get back.'

'Sure! Whatever! Let's just go!' Amy banged the door of Chicken HQ closed behind them and they took off into the sky after James Pond.

Chapter Four

Down in a burrow in the Deep Dark Woods, Thaddeus E. Fox drew back his chair and stood up. It was time to address the meeting.

He banged his silver-topped cane on the table.

'Friends,' he said, 'welcome to this session of the MOST WANTED Club.'

He surveyed the group. To his left was Tiny Tony Tiddles. Tiny Tony Tiddles was a small cat with a big attitude problem. He wore a black fedora on his head to make himself look like a gangster. Thaddeus E. Fox didn't like Tiny Tony. Tiddles was rude; he was resentful; he turned up at the burrow and helped himself to food without asking; he lounged on the cushions as though he owned the joint. Still, Thaddeus E. Fox had to admit, Tiny Tony Tiddles could be useful when it came to catching chickens.

Next to Tiny Tony Tiddles sat Kebab Claude, the big French poodle. Claude was as thick as one of his famous burgers, but he was ace at barbecuing chicken. That was why he was in the club.

Next to Kebab Claude perched the three members of the Pigeon-Poo Gang. Thaddeus E. Fox had a lot of respect for the Pigeon-Poo Gang. He admired the way they dressed. Of course they weren't as smart as *him* (Thaddeus always wore his old Eat'em College school uniform: top hat, tails and a silk waistcoat) but they had good taste for pigeons. Each had slicked back purple and grey feathers and a pair of cool shades. They were devious too. The pigeons had gone to the dark side and betrayed all their fellow bird kind. Thaddeus E. Fox particularly liked the way they conducted their criminal business by sludging their victims to death with poo that was so sticky it turned to concrete, then eating all their victims' food. It was vile; it was despicable; it was downright VILLAINOUS. He couldn't understand why more birds weren't like them.

'It's been a while,' Thaddeus remarked.

'Tell me about it, buddy!' Tiny Tony Tiddles said rudely. 'I spent the last six months with my paw in

a sling, thanks to those mangy chickens and that Professor Rooster dude.'

'Yes,' Thaddeus E. Fox sneered. 'I heard.'

Boo had led Tiny Tony Tiddles a merry dance across the rafters of Eat'em College during their first rescue mission. Tiny Tony had been so bedazzled by Boo's gymnastics moves that he had fallen off the wooden beams onto the floor and sprained his leg.

'You didn't come out of it too well yourself, Fox,' Tiny Tony snorted. 'Don't forget *you* got your whiskers covered in custard.' (That was thanks to Amy and her new wrestling move, the feather custy.)

'And mites,' Kebab Claude reminded him. 'Zey were all over your fur. You were scratching for weeks.' (That was down to Ruth and the mite blaster.)

Thaddeus E. Fox scowled at them. 'Moving swiftly on,' he snarled, 'there are two items on the agenda today.' He passed round some bits of paper.

AGENDA

1. Catching chicken
2. Catching more chicken

He waited patiently while everyone read it. 'I think it's time we organised another dinner . . .' he began.

'Forget it, Fox,' Tony Tiddles interrupted. 'I'm not going back to Eat'em College for another one of your get-togethers . . .'

'. . . at Bloodsucker Hall.' Thaddeus E. Fox stared him down.

'You mean where ze vampire mink lived?' Kebab Claude said in astonishment. 'Ze one zat sucked ze blood out of her birdie victims and turned zem into zombies?!' Countess Stella von Fangula was legendary amongst the predators of the Deep Dark Wood. They learned about her at school.

'Precisely.' Thaddeus E. Fox nodded. 'Except in one small, but significant respect, Claude: your use

of the past tense.' He looked solemn. 'Gentlemen, it is my great pleasure to inform you that the Countess Stella von Fangula has risen from the grave.'

'How?' Tiny Tony Tiddles demanded.

'Thanks to the extreme carelessness of a rooster at Fogsham Farm called Ichabod Comb,' the fox replied. Professor Rooster wasn't the only animal who had spies everywhere: so did Thaddeus E. Fox – ferrets, mostly, and weasels. He told the other members of the MOST WANTED Club the story.

'And you want to have dinner with *her*?' Tiddles cried. 'What? Are you nuts? What if she tries to eat *us*?'

Thaddeus E. Fox's patience snapped. 'If you don't shut up, *I'll* eat you.'

Tiny Tony Tiddles sank back on to the cushions.

'Think about it,' Thaddeus E. Fox said reasonably. 'It's not *us* Fangula wants to eat. It's roosters. And hens. And pheasants. And ducks. *Like we do.*' He paused. He could see he'd got their attention now.

'So what's the plan?' Tiny Tony sulked.

'We get von Fangula on side by asking her to become a member of the MOST WANTED Club,' Thaddeus replied. 'Then we arrange a dinner with her at Bloodsucker Hall. Claude can do the cooking. We'll help her raid the chicken sheds at Fogsham Farm: she loves killing chickens even more than we do. It's what she lives for. Well, sort of,' he added. It was hard to know how to talk about the undead.

'What about Professor Rooster and his squad?' Kebab Claude said. It wasn't just Thaddeus E. Fox who had been on the wrong end of the mite blaster once before: Kebab Claude had too.

'Trust me: those three kids are too chicken to take on Fangula and her zombie army,' Thaddeus scoffed. 'My bet is Rooster will concentrate on protecting the coops at Dudley Manor. And if the chickens do show up at Fogsham Farm, they'll end up on the dinner table with the rest of them.'

'With a few 'erbs and a sprinkle of salt,' Kebab Claude said dreamily.

'Indeed!' Thaddeus E. Fox grinned. 'I can just picture it now.'

Thaddeus licked his lips. 'So, gentlemen, are we agreed?'

'Oui,' Kebab Claude said.

'I guess so,' Tiny Tony said, 'but you'd better be right about Rooster and his team.'

'Coo, coo, coo!' The members of the Pigeon-Poo Gang were restless. Their leader addressed the meeting. 'What's in it for us?'

'You can strip out the chicken sheds.' Thaddeus E. Fox said. 'There's plenty of grain. The Fogsham Farm chickens have been hoarding it for the winter.'

The leader consulted with his members. 'We'll do it,' he agreed. 'As long as you keep Fangula under control.'

46

'You have my word,' Thaddeus E. Fox said solemnly. He opened a drawer in the table and took out a piece of expensive writing paper and a pen. Very carefully he began to write.

The Burrow
Deep Dark Woods
Dudley Estate

Dear Countess,

Welcome back! The MOST WANTED Club of villains would like to invite you to become a member of our exclusive dining club. To celebrate your return to the land of the living (or undead, whichever the case may be), we propose to hold a banquet in your honour at Bloodsucker Hall. The menu will consist of locally farmed chicken. We will bring our own BBQ sauce.

Your humble servant,
Thaddeus E. Fox

'Take this to von Fangula,' he told the Pigeon-Poo Gang.

The leader of the Pigeon-Poo Gang rolled the paper up in his beak, placed it in a tiny tube and strapped it to his leg.

'Tell her we'll be there tonight to get the preparations for the banquet under way.'

Thaddeus E. Fox showed the pigeons to the door of the burrow and watched as they took off and headed north towards the moor.

Chapter Five

'Are we nearly there yet?'

Amy flew over the moor after James Pond. They had been flying for ages; the flight-booster engines battling against the howling wind. The moor spread out beneath her, bleak and empty. Tendrils of fog swirled across the grass. Above her the sky was heavy with the threat of snow. Even though it was only mid afternoon the light was fading.

'I said, are we nearly there yet?' she repeated plaintively. The wind whipped her words away. James Pond didn't turn around.

Amy felt afraid. Normally she was tucked up at Chicken HQ by the time it got dark with Ruth and Boo in their cosy pallets of straw, or playing *Chicken World Wrestling 3* before bed while Boo brushed her feathers and Ruth recited her times tables. She glanced behind at Boo and Ruth. She hoped they were okay. Boo hadn't really wanted to be a chicken warrior in the first place. It was Amy who had persuaded her to complete their first mission. She had persuaded Ruth too, for that matter. If anything ever happened to either of them she would never forgive herself. The sooner James Pond got this over with, the better.

'There it is,' James Pond quacked.

Amy looked through her super-spec headset. Bloodsucker Hall was up ahead. It was even bigger and more desolate than she had imagined. The roof had caved in long ago and the walls were covered in thick vegetation. She scanned the building for signs of life. Three pigeons were sitting on a window ledge. They had their backs turned to her. For a horrible moment Amy thought it might be the Pigeon-Poo Gang. Then she told herself not to be silly: the Pigeon-Poo Gang wouldn't go anywhere near a vampire mink! She pushed up her headset and flew on.

The chickens travelled over the ruined church and the dry stone wall that ran round the perimeter of Fogsham Farm.

'Coming in to land!' James Pond quacked. He

began his descent to the farmyard. The chickens fluttered down after him.

Amy landed with a bump beside the chicken sheds.

'Thank goodness you're here!' An elderly rooster popped his head out of one of the sheds. His feathers were a rich silky black except for the ones on his neck and back, which were as white as snow. His comb and wattle (the dangly bit underneath his chin) were scarlet. 'Professor Rooster's elite chicken squad!' he said, nodding to himself. 'I'm Rossiter Brown.' Then he saw James Pond. 'I wasn't expecting four of you,' he frowned. 'The professor didn't say anything about a duck.'

'Don't worry, Rossiter, you're in good hands,' James Pond reassured him, stretching out a wing to give the rooster's a shake. 'I'm James Pond, Poultry Patrol. I've taken charge of the vampire slaying mission. You and your hens can rest easy in your hay now I'm here.'

Amy felt her cheeks glow. James Pond was being a massive big-head show-off again. She took a deep breath. *Just ignore him*, she told herself.

Rossiter Brown was looking at her for confirmation.

'That's right!' Amy grinned through gritted teeth. 'He's in charge!' She pulled a face behind James Pond's back.

'Well ... er ... good,' Rossiter Brown said. 'You'd better follow me, before the humans see your equipment. Not that there's much danger of that,' he added, 'they don't go out in this weather unless they have to.' He sighed. 'I'm having to do the dawn crow instead of Ichabod to remind the humans to give us our grain.' He shook his head. 'Poor Ichabod. Follow me, I'll show you where he was snatched.'

He led them towards a second shed. The chickens scuttled after him. James Pond brought up the rear with a swagger.

'This place gives me the creeps,' Boo said in a hushed voice.

'Me too!' Ruth whispered.

'Don't worry,' Amy said, 'we'll be out of here in no time.' She tried to sound bright. The farm was bleak and miserable. The paint on the sheds was peeling from the rain and the grass underfoot was scratched up and muddy. The place gave her the creeps too but someone had to be brave.

'That's right, ladies,' James Pond had overheard the conversation, 'there's nothing to fear: Pond is here.'

'My turn to need the sick bucket,' Boo groaned.

Amy couldn't help giggling. At least Boo had managed to keep her sense of humour! 'He's awful, isn't he?' she whispered back.

Rossiter Brown pushed open the door to the second shed. 'This is the juice shed,' he explained. 'This is where it happened, where that fiend attacked Ichabod.'

Inside the shed it was even darker. Something scratchy squeezed between Amy's toes. She looked down. The floor was covered with sawdust.

'We put it down to mop up the blood,' Rossiter Brown said. 'We swept up the china thimble as well. We didn't want anyone else cutting themselves in case Fangula returned.'

Amy looked round the interior of The Bloodless Hen. There were stools for the chickens to sit on; upturned crates served as tables and there was even

53

a dartboard hanging on the wall in one corner. It reminded her a little bit of the barn where she used to play at Perrin's Farm before she had become an elite chicken warrior. The juice shed might have been a fun place to hang out before Ichabod Comb was attacked. Now it was just dead scary.

'Hmm, a CD rack,' Ruth had gone over to the bar to investigate.

'What's a CD rack?' Amy asked.

'It's what humans used in the old days to store their music,' Ruth explained. 'Now they do it electronically.'

Amy was baffled, but she went over to have a look anyway.

The other side of the bar was hollowed out and divided into compartments. Lined up inside each of the compartments were stacks of plastic cups and bottles of worm juice. 'Where were the rest of you,' Ruth asked, 'when it happened?'

'In our sleeping quarters,' Rossiter told her, 'in another shed. We have five sheds in total: The Bloodless Hen, the shop, the leisure centre, the school and the sleeping coop. The rest of us went back there.

It was just after nine. Ichabod said he'd stay here and clear up. Fangula must have sneaked in when we weren't looking.' He shook his head sadly. 'That was the last we saw of him.'

'Didn't you think it was odd when he didn't come back?' Ruth asked.

'No,' Rossiter replied. 'Ichabod told me he'd sleep here. I was a little worried about it, I must admit, but he insisted. He had an early start the next morning. He didn't want to disturb us.'

'Do you know how Fangula woke up in the first place?' Boo enquired.

'I think it must have been Ichabod's doing, I'm afraid,' Rossiter sighed. 'We warned him, of course. When he first came to Fogsham Farm before Christmas, we told him about the curse. We told him not to go to the hall.'

'Why did he, then?' asked Amy.

'Ichabod was brave,' said Rossiter. 'He'd been in the army – as a mascot for the humans. He said he didn't believe in the curse. That's why he went. Only when he got there he cut his foot on a broken slate.' Rossiter shook his head sadly. 'He told me afterwards he'd never felt so scared in his life before. He said it was as if the house had laid a trap for him.'

Amy felt sorry for Ichabod Comb, but she couldn't help thinking that he was an awful idiot. Why couldn't he just stay put at Fogsham Farm like all the other chickens? It was like one of those scary shows she'd seen on the BBC (Bird Broadcasting Corporation) where a bunch of silly teenage chickens went down into the basement in the dark even though they'd been told not to by the grown-ups.

James Pond was peering out of the window. Amy followed his gaze. It was almost completely dark. And darkness was when the Countess Stella von Fangula would rise from her grave.

'We should get back to the sleeping coop and secure the doors,' James Pond said. 'We'll get up early and finish the job in the morning when Fangula's safely back in her coffin.'

Rossiter Brown gave a little cough. 'I'm dreadfully sorry,' he said, 'but we can't squeeze you all in, not with your equipment. I don't suppose you'd mind

 57

sleeping in here tonight? There's a hammer and nails and a few spare planks of wood to make the place safe. We can lend you some straw.'

Amy looked at Boo. Her face was stricken with fear. Amy was just about to suggest that the three of them should snuggle up with Rossiter and the other chickens and leave James Pond to guard the equipment in The Bloodless Hen when James Pond opened his beak.

'That's fine,' he said. 'Amy and Ruth, you go with Rossiter and get the straw. Boo, check for holes. Von Fangula must have got in somehow.'

'And what are you going to do,' Amy said indignantly, 'apart from boss everyone else around?'

'Fix myself something to eat,' James Pond said. 'I've got a vampire to slay at dawn. Besides, I'm in charge. It's my job to boss everyone else around.'

'It's okay, Amy,' Boo said in a low voice. 'I don't mind doing what he says, as long as we get out of here tomorrow in one piece.'

'I agree,' Ruth whispered. 'Let's just leave it.'

Amy took a deep breath. 'Okay,' she hissed.

'But if anything goes wrong, I'll personally kick James Pond's butt.' She trudged across the freezing farmyard with Ruth to collect the straw.

Chapter Six

The rest of the evening went better; to begin with, anyway. Once Amy and Ruth had returned with the straw, they arranged it into two neat piles: one for them and one for James Pond, while James Pond went round with Boo securing the doors and windows with the hammer and nails and patching up any holes in the planks that a mink could sneak through. Then the chickens helped themselves to some food. Luckily there was plenty of grain and grub scratchings to go round. Amy felt relieved. Her tummy had been grumbling for hours. It was hungry work being a chicken warrior.

When they finished their tea, Ruth laid out the mite blaster on one of the upturned crates.

'What are you doing?' asked Amy.

'I'm removing the mite tube and replacing it with a garlic one,' Ruth explained. 'Just in case Fangula *does* show up tonight.'

'You don't think she will, do you?' Boo asked anxiously.

'Of course not,' Amy reassured her. 'But Ruth's right. It won't hurt to be on the safe side.' Being on the safe side was something her mother was always very keen on. Amy had never paid much attention before, particularly when it came to wrestling. But something told her that now was a good time to start.

'Put this one behind the bar, would you, Amy?' Ruth gently withdrew the mite tube from the blaster. 'Be careful not to drop it, though. We don't want mites all over the floor.'

'Don't worry, I've got it.' Amy took the mite tube from Ruth. She inched her way gingerly behind the bar.

'Keep it upright, Amy,' Ruth advised. 'So none of the little beasts escapes.'

'Okay.' There wasn't much space what with all the bottles and cups. Amy propped the mite tube up between two bottles of worm juice. It would be fine there as long as no one bumped it. She squeezed her way back round the bar to join the others.

James Pond had finished hammering. 'You won't need that.' He said, taking a look at the garlic blaster. 'Fangula can't get in.' He closed the curtains.

Amy glanced around the chicken shed. Maybe working with James Pond wasn't so bad after all. She had to admit he'd done a good job of securing the shed. The door bristled with nails. So did the window. So did the felt roof. It would take an army of zombie chickens to get through them. And Fangula didn't have an army this time: only Ichabod Comb. She rustled her feathers and jumped onto the hay. 'Let's get some sleep.'

'Okay.' Boo smoothed her feathery boots and joined her.

'I'm eggshausted!' Ruth said. She laid the garlic blaster next to the straw and took her glasses off. Then she jumped in beside the others. The three chickens snuggled down. They heard a satisfied quack as James Pond retired to his bed for the night.

'I feel a lot safer with all those nails Pond hammered in,' Boo admitted.

'Me too,' Ruth agreed. 'Nothing can get through

that lot. Not even a vampire mink and her zombies.'

Amy grunted. She felt safer too but she didn't want James Pond to know.

BANG! The door rattled.

The chickens jumped.

'What was that?' Boo whispered.

'Probably just the wind,' James Pond replied. 'Go to sleep.'

BUMP!

'There it is again!' Ruth hissed.

The straw rustled as James Pond got out of bed. They heard the soft swish of his tail as he went around the shed checking the reinforcements.

BASH!

Amy gulped. It wasn't the wind. It sounded more like someone or something was throwing rocks at the door.

'It must be Fangula!' Amy squawked.

'And Ichabod Comb!' squealed Ruth.

'What shall we do?' screeched Boo.

'Don't panic,' James Pond ordered. 'I've told you: they can't get in. The nails will hold them.'

BANG!

BUMP!

BASH!

The noises came again in quick succession.

'Try telling them that!' Amy shrieked.

BANG!

BUMP!

BASH!

The chickens crept out of the straw. Ruth reached for her glasses and pushed them up her beak. She grabbed the garlic blaster.

'Can you see Fangula?' Amy whispered.

'No, it's too dark.' James Pond was crouching by the window.

BANG!

BUMP!

BASH!

CRASH!

A missile flew at the door. Two of the nails pinged out.

'Barn-it!' he swore softly. 'They're stronger than I thought.'

'What are we going to do?' Boo sobbed.

'There's only one thing we can do.' James Pond drew the slim case containing Vladimir's Vampire Slayer from its holster. He screwed the plastic cylinder onto the handle and slotted the pencil in.

'What, you mean you're going to try and kill Fangula NOW?' Amy squeaked. 'But what if you miss? She'll suck our blood out and turn us into zombies!'

'I won't miss,' James Pond said calmly. 'I have perfect aim. I just need one of you to distract her so she doesn't see me until it's too late.'

The chickens looked at one another, aghast.

'You could do some gymnastics, Boo,' suggested Amy.

'I'm too scared.' Boo's legs were shaking. 'How about you do your feather dusty instead, Amy?' she pleaded.

The feather dusty was one of Amy's best wrestling moves. It consisted of rubbing her tummy feathers in dirt and smothering her opponent's face with dust. Normally Amy would have agreed. But to try out the

feather dusty on Fangula would be suicide. Fangula would sink her gnashers straight into her neck, Amy was sure of it. 'Er . . . I don't think so.' She trembled.

CRUMP!

Something bounced off the window. A crack appeared in the glass pane.

'Could you just decide?' James Pond said crossly. 'Only we haven't got much time.'

'We'll use this.' Ruth waved the garlic blaster. 'It'll hold her off for a bit. The garlic's crushed.'

'Good,' James Pond said coolly. He gave a little bow. 'When you're ready, ladies, we'll do some vampire slaying!' He stepped behind the bar and ducked down out of sight.

The chickens hid behind one of the wooden crates.

'LET US IN!' a voice screeched. 'WE'RE STARVING.'

A blood-curdling roar went up. 'WE WANT FOOD! WE WANT FOOD! WE WANT FOOD!'

'Flap!' screamed Boo. 'There's loads of them. Fangula must have munched some more chickens!'

Amy frowned. 'Where did she get them from?

There aren't any other farms around here.'

'I don't know, do I?' Boo wailed. 'Maybe she raided the sleeping coop!'

'But we would have heard something!' Amy insisted.

'It doesn't matter now.' Ruth clutched the garlic blaster. 'Amy, get me some more garlic. There's another tube on top of the bar. I've got a feeling we're going to need it.'

Amy rushed towards the bar. In her haste she tripped over one of the bar stools.

'Ouch!' Amy took a dive and bashed her head on the CD rack. The garlic tube teetered on the top. She flung out a wing and caught it. 'Phew!' she said, 'that was lucky!'

SMASH!

Uh? Amy examined the garlic tube. It definitely wasn't broken. And nor was the window (not yet, anyway). So what had made the smashing noise? Amy peered over the top of the bar. Her eyes grew round. 'Oops,' she whispered. It was the mite tube! It must have fallen out when she hit her head on the CD rack. Now it lay in two pieces on the floor. 'Oh dear,' she said. The mites had escaped.

'TICKTICKTICKTICKTICKTICK!' A column of tiny insects marched their way determinedly towards James Pond's tail feathers.

'Aarrrggghhhh!' James Pond emerged from behind the CD rack scratching his backside frantically. 'Look what you've done, you hopeless hen!' he shouted at Amy.

But there was no time for Amy to apologise or to tell him it was just an accident and not to call her

rude names like 'hopeless hen', because at that point everything happened at once.

BANG! The door flew open.

SPLOOSH! Ruth fired the garlic blaster.

'DUCK!' James Pond raised the vampire slayer.

SMASH! Something hurtled through the window.

BAM! It landed on James Pond's wing, knocking him sideways.

WHOOSH! The pencil shot out of the vampire slayer towards Boo and Ruth.

FLUMP! Amy flung herself on top of them.

CLUNK! The pencil clattered harmlessly on the table.

'What the peck was that?' James Pond sat up, dazed. He was still scratching.

Amy stared at the missile. It looked strangely familiar. It had four legs like a stool but no seat. She'd definitely seen it somewhere before . . .

Suddenly she remembered. Her eyes widened. 'Hold up, everyone!' she shouted. 'It's not Fangula.'

Just then a wizened old chicken's face appeared at the door, smothered in minced garlic. Behind it was

an army of other wizened old chickens' faces.

'Give me back my Zimmer frame!' a voice screeched.

Amy pushed her way past Boo and Ruth. 'Granny Wishbone!' she squawked. 'What are you doing here?'

Chapter Seven

Down in a dungeon in the ruins of Bloodsucker Hall, Thaddeus E. Fox drew back his chair and stood up. It was time to address the meeting.

He banged his silver-topped cane on the table.

'Friends,' he said, 'welcome to this session of the MOST WANTED Club.'

He surveyed the group with some satisfaction. The Pigeon-Poo Gang had settled to sleep high up on a ledge in the wall. Tiny Tony Tiddles and Kebab Claude sprawled in their chairs, yawning. They were all too tired from their long journey to give him any trouble tonight. Instead he was able to give his attention to the newest member of the MOST WANTED Club: the Countess Stella von Fangula. The countess sat opposite him in her scarlet cloak, looking very glamorous. For a mink who was over two hundred years old, Thaddeus thought, she looked pretty darned good.

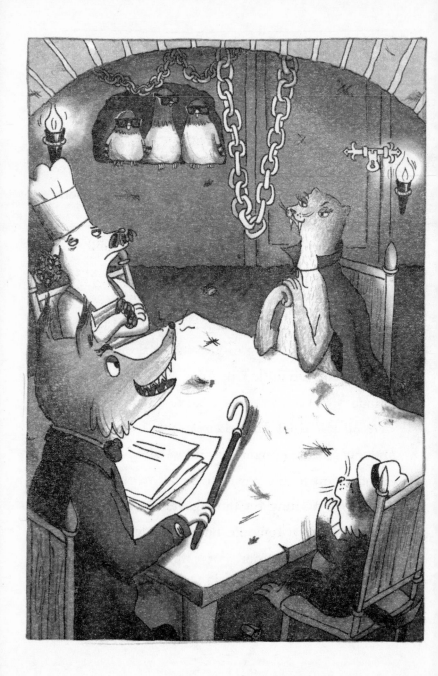

Thaddeus drew his tailcoat around him for warmth. The only drawback to having the meeting at Bloodsucker Hall was that it wasn't as cosy as his burrow in the Deep Dark Woods. The dungeon was below ground so at least it had a roof but damp still penetrated the walls. Torches burned in great braziers; the earth floor was littered with bugs and beetles, and the air smelled musty. Rusty chains hung from the ceiling. They clanked faintly when anyone came in or out through the heavy iron door. But they were minor details, thought Thaddeus. Soon they would be feasting on the chickens of Fogsham Farm. He could put up with a damp dungeon for a day or two.

'I am sure we would all like to thank the countess for her . . . er . . . wonderful hospitality,' Thaddeus E. Fox began.

'There's nothing very wonderful about it as far as I can see,' Tiny Tony Tiddles said rudely. 'It sucks, like her.'

'But darling,' the countess protested in her husky voice, 'it was such short notice! I only got your message a couple of hours ago. There wasn't much time to clean up before you arrived.'

Thaddeus glanced at his fob watch. It was six o' clock. It had taken them all day to get from the Deep Dark Woods to Bloodsucker Hall. The Pigeon-Poo Gang had been waiting for them when they arrived. It turned out they had only just managed to deliver their message to the countess. Thaddeus cursed himself for forgetting that vampires didn't get up until darkness fell. He should have waited until tomorrow so that the countess could prepare properly for their arrival.

'Where are we gonna sleep?' Tiny Tiddles persisted. 'It's filthy in here.'

'You can have my coffin if you like,' the countess offered. 'I only use it in the daytime.' She smiled, revealing two rows of sharp white teeth. 'We can take turns.'

'No thanks,' said Tony.

'I'm hungry,' Kebab Claude drooled. 'What's for supper?'

'I'll ask Ichabod,' the countess said. 'Ichabod . . .'

The zombie chicken appeared.

'Yes, m'lady?'

'What's for supper?'

Ichabod tilted his head back and looked craftily up at the ledge. 'Pigeon, m'lady,' he said.

There was an alarmed cooing from overhead.

'Ichabod!' the countess admonished. 'The poo pigeons are our guests. You will have to give our friends something else to eat.'

'All right, m'lady.' Ichabod limped out. 'I'll see what I can find in the kitchen.'

'There are two items on the agenda this evening,' Thaddeus E. Fox said. He passed round some bits of paper.

AGENDA
1. Catching chicken
2. Catching more chicken

'May I suggest a third?' the countess said.

'Of course.' Thaddeus offered her a pen.

The countess wrote in beautiful handwriting:

3. Drinking rooster blood

Tiny Tony and Kebab Claude exchanged glances.

'Bleeeaaaarrrcchhh!' said Tiny Tony.

The countess ignored him. 'It's so lovely to have company after all these years,' she said to Thaddeus. She clapped her paws together in delight. 'And so kind of you to arrange a banquet for me! I do so hope there will be rooster blood on the menu!' She batted her eyelashes. 'It's my favourite drink.'

'Are there many roosters at Fogsham Farm?' Thaddeus asked.

'I don't think so,' the countess said sadly. 'Only Ichabod and one other, and I've already drunk all of Ichabod's blood. I was so *thirsty*, you see, after all those years in the coffin.'

'Can't you drink 'ens' blood?' Kebab Claude asked.

'I can,' said the countess. 'I can drink any bird's blood . . .'

There was a rustling of feathers from overhead.

'. . . but it just doesn't taste as *good* as rooster.'

'We'll help you catch the other rooster,' Thaddeus promised. He scratched his whiskers thoughtfully. 'What are the fortifications like at the chicken sheds? Are there any humans around?'

The countess shook her head. 'I didn't see any last night,' she said. 'I don't think they go out after dark.'

'How did you get in?' demanded Tiny Tony.

'There was a hole in the back of the shed. I waited until all the other chickens had left and then I popped in and introduced myself to Ichabod. I wanted to thank him personally for waking me up,' said the countess fondly.

'Sounds like a stroll in the park,' Tiny Tony remarked.

'Well, yes,' the countess agreed, 'but then the chickens weren't exactly *expecting* me. They might be more careful next time.'

'PHWA HA HA HA,' Thaddeus let out his evil

laugh. 'Don't you worry about the other chickens, Countess. They're too stupid to protect themselves.'

'Unless they get Professor Rooster and his squad in,' Tiny Tony commented.

'Shut up, Tony,' Thaddeus snapped. 'I've already told you they won't come.'

'Professor Rooster?' the countess repeated. 'He sounds tasty. Do tell.'

'He's a rooster we've had trouble with at Dudley Manor,' Thaddeus explained. 'He put a team of kid combat chickens together to protect the coop, but I'm pretty sure they won't risk coming as far as the moor.'

'Pity,' said the countess thoughtfully. 'I like a feisty chicken. Their blood gives me more zip.'

Just then Ichabod returned, carrying a tray.

'Dinner is served, m'lady,' he said.

'What is it?' Tiny Tony Tiddles asked.

'Bat wing stew with mashed bugs,' Ichabod said proudly.

'Delicious, darling!' the countess took a bite. 'Now, when is the banquet to be?' she asked Thaddeus.

'We'll raid the coop tomorrow night,' Thaddeus

replied, crunching loudly on bug shells. 'And then we shall have our feast before the humans wake up to the fact that their chickens have gone.' He picked a bit of bat wing out of his teeth and laughed. 'PHWA-HA-HA-HA-HA! Those chickens had better start praying.'

Chapter Eight

'The Chicken Zimmer Frame Throwing Championships?' Amy repeated for the umpteenth time. 'I still can't believe it!'

At first light the next morning the chickens made their way out of The Bloodless Hen chicken shed. James Pond waddled ahead of them. He was still scratching. And he had a huge bump on his head, like an egg.

'Shhhh,' he hissed. 'We don't want to wake the other chickens, especially not Wishbone and her cronies.'

The chickens followed cautiously. Amy was behind James Pond, carrying the Emergency Chicken Pack. Next came Boo with the flight boosters in case they had to make a quick getaway. Ruth brought up the rear with the super-spec headsets.

'I didn't even know there *was* a Chicken Zimmer Frame Throwing Championship,' Ruth sighed.

It turned out that the bunch of bloodthirsty granny hens they had taken to be Fangula's zombie army were at Fogsham Farm for a different reason.

'Just our luck that Granny Wishbone turns out to be the Chicken Zimmer Frame Throwing Record Holder,' Boo said crossly.

'And that this year's competition is at Bleakley Fogsham!' Amy complained. Her cheeks glowed red. She was starving! And her neck ached from lying on the floor. Once the grannies had breached their defences and got inside The Bloodless Hen, they'd scoffed all the grain, munched all the grub scratchings, drunk all the worm juice and stolen all the straw. Then they'd snored like pigs all night.

'*And* that they saw the ad in the newspaper!' Boo added miserably. Apparently the grannies, who lived at the edge of the moor in a ramshackle smallholding, had seen an advert for the Fogsham Farm bed and breakfast in an old newspaper and decided the desolate chicken sheds looked just the place for a weekend break. They'd flown there by seagull, in return for eggs, which they'd stolen from

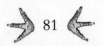

some younger hens who lived next door to the smallholding.

'Hurry up!' James Pond snapped. He had reached the dry stone wall.

The chickens flapped after him. They threw the equipment over the top of the wall, hoisted themselves up and dropped down on the other side.

'This is the path.' James Pond led on.

'How about giving us a hand with something?' Amy panted. The Emergency Chicken Pack was heavy. James Pond had insisted on them bringing the hammer just in case. And there were all sorts of other things in there as well, rattling about.

'I'm fine thanks,' James Pond said. 'Besides, the exercise will do you good.'

Amy's cheeks glowed even redder. She threw the Emergency Chicken Pack on her back and struggled on.

Soon they reached the ruined church. Amy hurried past. The church was creepy. Gravestones stuck up from the heather. They towered above the chickens like enormous bird bills.

'What if some of Fangula's zombies from 1887 are buried here?' Boo whispered. 'What if she summons them from the grave?'

'*She* won't get the chance if *you* get a move on,' James Pond said impatiently. 'That's the whole point. Here.' They had reached the rusty iron gates of Bloodsucker Hall. He hopped through.

The chickens followed, one by one. They gazed upwards.

'Bloodsucker Hall!' Ruth breathed.

Ahead of them, through a jungle of bushes and tall grass, stood the hall. It looked even scarier from the ground than it had from the air. Most of the roof had fallen in. A tangle of ivy hung around the derelict building like green witches' hair. The windows were as black as the eye sockets of a skull. Amy couldn't get the idea out of her head that the house was watching them.

'Come on.' James Pond pushed his way through the thicket, the chickens dodging behind.

'Can you hear that?' Boo whispered.

'What?' Amy strained her ears.

'Nothing,' Boo said. 'There's no noise at all.'

Amy realised she was right. No birds sang. There were no bees or butterflies or bugs. The place was as quiet as a grave.

Eventually they reached the steps which led up to the great front door. Amy swallowed. Either side of the steps stood hideous statues of stricken birds. Crouching over each one of them – fangs bared – was the slender stone figure of Countess Stella von Fangula.

'That's where she was killed,' Ruth whispered. 'At the top of the steps.'

'The question is, where is she buried?' Amy said. She hoped James Pond would get this over with quickly.

'Over here.' James Pond had a pen in his wing. The tip of it glowed amber.

'What's that?' Boo asked.

'Vladimir's Vampire Tracker, of course,' James Pond said. 'The redder it gets, the closer we are to the coffin.' He held the pen in front of him and trudged off around the building. They approached a tangle of

thorny bushes. 'It's in here.' The pen shone scarlet.

'We can't go in there,' Boo said. 'We'll get cut to ribbons.' The thorns were as big and sharp as a lion's claws.

'We don't have to!' James Pond said. He replaced the pen in the holster and pulled out a green plastic bottle with a spray nozzle.

VLADIMIR'S THORN KILLER – TACKLES THORNS IN AN INSTANT!

He held it out and squeezed the nozzle.

PUFF!

The thorn bushes evaporated.

The chickens regarded him with awe. 'I wish I'd thought of that!' Ruth said.

'There it is!' Amy nudged her friends. She pointed to a fresh mound of earth.

The grave looked as if it had recently been dug and refilled. There were chicken footprints in it where the soil had been hastily trodden down.

Ichabod! thought Amy.

The chickens put down their equipment and approached the gravestone cautiously. With one wing Amy traced the letters carved into the stone. She might not be a good reader, but she could manage this.

She withdrew her wing, shivering. The stone was ice cold to the touch.

'Wait, there's more!' Ruth brushed away some soil from the base of the gravestone.

Amy read the words slowly, repeating them to herself until she understood them.

TO ET-ERN-IT-Y AND BE-YOND!

'Not if we've got anything to do with it!' she muttered.

'Not if *I've* got anything to do with it, you mean,' James Pond corrected her. 'Let's get to work.' He sat down.

Amy regarded him with dislike. 'What are you waiting for?' she said impatiently.

'We've got to dig her up,' James Pond retorted. 'Or rather, you three do.'

'What?' the chickens squawked.

'I'm in charge of this operation,' James Pond snapped. 'I give the orders around here.'

'Don't you have a gadget to dig her up with?' Ruth asked hopefully.

'Only these.' James Pond reached into his holster and handed the chickens three teaspoons.

Amy snatched hers crossly. 'What if we refuse?' she demanded.

'Then I'll tell Professor Rooster you asked me to complete the mission,' James Pond said lightly. 'Don't think I haven't worked out you hens didn't *really* want to do it.'

The three chickens looked at one another guiltily.

'You can't tell him,' retorted Amy. 'We don't have the laptop.'

'I don't *need* the laptop,' James Pond boasted, 'I'm Poultry Patrol, remember? I'm one of the few birds who knows where Professor Rooster's secret hideout is.'

Amy glowered at him.

James Pond gave his tail feathers a scratch. 'And if I *do* tell Professor Rooster, I reckon he'll ask me to hang around a bit longer as team leader to help you hens out, which I wouldn't mind doing.' He shrugged. 'Your choice.'

Boo and Ruth looked at Amy uncertainly.

'Team talk,' Amy said.

The chickens went into a huddle.

'We *could* slay Fangula ourselves,' Amy said defiantly. 'And tell Pond to push off.'

'We've been through this, Amy,' Boo sighed.

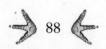

'None of us want to do it.'

Ruth nodded. 'I'd rather dig her up and leave it to Pond,' she said.

Amy felt cross: not with Boo and Ruth but with herself. She knew they didn't blame her for not being as brave as James Pond, but that didn't stop her blaming herself. 'Oh, all right,' she said eventually.

The chickens set to work. Luckily chickens are good at digging. It wasn't long before they had dug a deep hole.

DWANG! Amy's teaspoon struck something hard. 'That's it! The iron coffin!'

The chickens swept the remaining soil off with their wings.

'Stand aside, ladies.' James Pond jumped down beside them. He wedged a stout stick under the coffin lid and tried to lever it open. The coffin lid remained firmly shut. He tried again. Nothing happened.

Amy brightened a little. Now was her chance to show James Pond she was better at something than he was! 'Here, let me,' she seized the stick and shoved him out of the way. Gripping the stick in both wings,

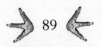

she pushed down with all her strength. There was a grinding sound as the lock broke.

'Good job, Amy!' Boo and Ruth congratulated her.

'I must have loosened it,' James Pond growled. Quickly he assembled Vladimir's Vampire Slayer. 'Lift the lid up.'

The three chickens did as they were told. Even Amy could see now wasn't the time for a squabble. She placed the tips of her wings between the coffin and its lid and heaved.

'Put your backs into it!' James Pond hissed.

CCCCRRREEEEAAAAKKKK! The lid inched open on its rusty hinges until it reached the top of its arc. It fell back against the wall of earth.

The chickens peered in. Amy felt a shiver of fear ruffle her feathers.

Inside the coffin was the body of the Countess Stella von Fangula.

Chapter Nine

'She's not breathing!' Boo whispered.

The vampire mink lay snugly on the coffin's red velvet lining in a blood red cloak, her eyes tightly closed.

'That's because she's dead,' Amy reminded her.

'No she's not,' Ruth objected. 'Technically she's *undead*. That's why we need to kill her.'

Amy felt confused.

'So far, so good,' James Pond's voice cut in. 'All I have to do now is drive the stake through her heart.' He squinted at the countess's body. 'I need to get the right angle. I'm too close here.'

The chickens clambered out of the grave after James Pond. To Amy's surprise he was rummaging in the Emergency Chicken Pack. He pulled out some overalls and a pair of rubber boots. 'In case it gets messy,' he said, putting them on.

Amy shot a quick glance at her friends. Boo's face

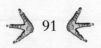

was green. She looked as if she was about to be sick. Even Ruth's feathers were definitely whiter than normal. 'Er . . . you don't mind if we have a break, do you?' Amy asked. 'That digging was hard work.'

'Haven't got the stomach for it?' James Pond guessed. 'Don't worry. You hens don't need to watch. I'll be done in a minute.' He pulled on the overalls and leaned over the grave.

The chickens retreated to the long grass.

'La la la la la!' Amy covered her ears with her wings.

'Do be do be do!' Boo did the same.

'Once twelve is twelve, twice twelve is twenty-four, three twelves are thirty-six . . .' So did Ruth.

BAM!

The chickens stopped singing and chanting. They hugged one another with relief.

'Phew!' Ruth said. 'I'm glad that's over.'

'Me too!' Boo took a deep breath.

'Now we can go back to Chicken HQ and wait for the next mission,' Amy said. 'Hooray!'

They hopped out of the long grass.

'Er, where's James Pond?' Ruth asked.

Three pairs of chicken eyes scanned the ground in vain: there was no sign of James Pond. Instead a four-legged object occupied his spot beside the grave. It looked like a stool without the seat.

'Oh no!' Amy groaned. 'It's Granny Wishbone's Zimmer frame!'

'She must have been practising for the championships!' Boo cried in horror.

'She's whacked Pond again!' Ruth shrieked. 'She's knocked him in!'

Amy, Boo and Ruth scuttled towards the grave and peered over the edge.

James Pond lay face down in the coffin on top of the Countess von Fangula. Beside him was Vladimir's Vampire Slayer. It was still loaded with the sharpened pencil.

He never got to fire it, Amy realised. The noise they'd heard was the sound of Granny Wishbone's Zimmer frame cracking James Pond on the head.

'He's unconscious!' Boo squealed.

'Which means Fangula's still alive!' squawked Amy.

'I mean undead. Well, whatever.' She gasped. A drop of blood oozed from a gash above James Pond's right eye where the Zimmer frame had hit him. It slid towards Countess von Fangula's lips.

'Let's be scientific about this,' Ruth said in a trembling voice. 'Pond's a duck, not a chicken. Maybe vampire minks don't like duck blood.'

'But Professor Rooster said Fangula would kill any bird!' Boo howled. 'And she killed the pheasants in 1887. Why not a duck?'

'Hmm . . .' Ruth scratched her head. 'Well then, it's daylight. She can't rise from the grave in daylight.'

Just then there was a flash of lightning followed by a huge clap of thunder.

Amy glanced fearfully at the sky. It was getting dark, really dark. Dense black clouds rolled across the moor, completely blotting out the light. Very soon it was pitch black.

'Got any other ideas, Ruth?' Amy swallowed.

Ruth shook her head. 'Nope. I think Pond's had it.'

'We've got to get him out of there!' Boo screamed.

'I'll do it!' Amy jumped into the coffin.

She grabbed James Pond round the middle and lifted him up.

DRIP! The drop of blood fell from James Pond's head and trickled between Countess von Fangula's lips. Her snout began to twitch.

'She's waking up!' screamed Boo. 'Quick, Amy!'

Amy bent her knees and hurled James Pond out of the grave. She started to clamber out. Suddenly she felt something grip her round the ankle. She glanced down. It was the Countess von Fangula's paw! 'Help!' she screeched.

'Get the garlic blaster, Ruth!' Boo cried. 'I'll help Amy.' She leaned over the edge of the grave, took hold of Amy's wings with hers and tried to tug her out.

The countess's grip tightened. Amy felt her leg being tugged in the other direction: towards the countess's mouth.

'Oh no you don't!' Boo hauled on her wings.

'Ow!' Amy cried. She was being stretched!

'Hang on, Amy!' Boo shouted.

Amy felt a glimmer of hope. Boo was strong from

all her gymnastics practice. And even though Boo was terrified, Amy knew she wouldn't let her be eaten by a vampire mink without putting up a fight. That's why Boo's special skill was perseverance: you could rely on her in a chicken crisis not to let you down.

CRASH! BANG! Amy could hear Ruth going through the Emergency Chicken Pack. 'The garlic blaster's not in here!' Ruth wailed. 'I left it in The Bloodless Hen!'

'There must be something else!' Boo insisted.

The countess's mouth opened. She raised her head towards Amy's foot. Amy kicked and struggled. The paw gripped harder. It closed round her ankle like a steel trap.

'I've found something.' Ruth appeared at the grave opening next to Boo. She was bearing a small metal can in one wing.

Amy squinted at it.

MITE BLASTER GREASE

'It will make your leg slippery, Amy.' Ruth reached into the grave and squirted some towards Fangula's paw.

Amy felt the greasy spray on her leg.

'Pull, Boo!' Ruth shouted.

Boo braced herself and gave Amy's wing a strong tug.

POP! Amy shot out of the grave on top of Boo. The mite blaster grease had worked!

'Let's get out of here!' Amy picked up James Pond and threw him over her shoulder. Boo and Ruth gathered up the equipment and raced after her.

The chickens stumbled towards the rusty iron gates of Bloodsucker Hall.

The storm was still raging. The sky was black.

Just then Granny Wishbone limped past them through the grass in the opposite direction.

'He-he!' she cried, spying the Zimmer frame. 'Another world record throw!' She hobbled towards it.

'No!' Amy yelled.

'Don't!' Boo begged.

'There's a vampire mink on the loose!' Ruth warned her.

'Don't be daft.' Granny Wishbone made her way in the direction of the grave.

The chickens watched in horror. A paw appeared over the side, followed by another. The Countess von Fangula had risen from her coffin.

'Ichabod!' she called. 'Where are you, darling? We have chickens to kill.'

'Yes, m'lady.' From out of the darkness came the zombie rooster. Amy stared at him in dismay. Most of his feathers had fallen off and goo dripped from his beak. He walked stiffly to meet Granny Wishbone.

'Get out of my way!' Granny Wishbone walloped him. More feathers fell off.

'I like a feisty chicken,' the countess laughed. She crept towards Granny Wishbone. 'How would you like to be the leader of my new zombie army?' She pounced.

Just then a crack appeared in the clouds. A ray of sunshine lit up Bloodsucker Hall.

'Aaarrrgggh!' the countess screamed. She dragged Granny Wishbone back into the grave.

THUNK! The coffin lid closed.

Ichabod Comb vanished into the mist.

All that remained was the Zimmer frame.

Chapter Ten

Down in a dungeon in the ruins of Bloodsucker Hall, Thaddeus E. Fox drew back his chair and stood up. It was time to address the meeting.

He banged his silver-topped cane on the table.

'Friends,' he said, 'welcome to this emergency session of the MOST WANTED Club.'

He surveyed the group with some annoyance. Tiny Tony Tiddles was looking insufferably smug. The cat had 'I told you so' written all over his face. Kebab Claude seemed anxious. The poodle kept casting his eyes nervously at the door as if he was expecting someone to charge in and blast him with mites at any moment. And the Pigeon-Poo Gang had retreated to the ledge again after a close shave with the newest recruit to the countess's zombie army – Granny Wishbone.

Only the Countess von Fangula remained unruffled. She drew her cloak around her shoulders and smiled at him.

Thaddeus smiled back. He relaxed a little. There were villains, he thought, and there were super villains. He and the countess both fell into the second category.

'There are four items on the agenda this evening,' Thaddeus said. He handed round some bits of paper.

AGENDA
1. Catching chicken
2. Catching more chicken
3. Drinking rooster blood
4. Defeating our enemies

'Let's start with item four. Countess, describe what happened this morning before you turned Granny Wishbone into a zombie. I want every last detail.'

The countess leaned forward. She spoke in a throaty whisper. 'I was fast asleep, darling, when I heard a noise. I think it was someone opening my coffin lid.

Then a little while later I sensed the delicious taste of duck blood on my lips . . .'

'Duck blood?' Tiny Tony repeated. 'You sure about that?'

'Darling Teeny Tiny Tony,' the countess said mildly, 'I have drunk enough blood in my time to recognise which bird it is from. May I continue?'

'Please,' said Thaddeus.

'Then it went dark because of the storm,' said the countess, 'and I woke up to find that there was a chicken in my coffin . . .'

The countess told the rest of her story.

'So there were three chickens in all?' Tiny Tony said.

'Yes.'

'Can you remember what they looked like, Countess?' Thaddeus asked. He needed to be sure if it really was Professor Rooster's squad before he decided what to do.

The countess thought for a moment. 'The one in the coffin was small with red cheeks and a fluffy tummy. The one who pulled her out had honey-

coloured boots. And the third one – the one with the grease squirt – she was definitely wearing specs.'

'Professor Rooster's elite chicken squad,' Tiny Tony said triumphantly. He curled his lip. 'I told you so, Fox. I knew Rooster would send them to Fogsham Farm. I said so, didn't I?'

'Shut up,' Thaddeus growled.

Tiny Tony was not to be silenced. 'Did you get a look at the duck, Countess?' he asked.

'It was a mallard,' the Countess said. 'It had a bow tie.'

'James Pond,' Tiny Tony spat, 'the dude from Poultry Patrol. That's all we need!'

'Poultry Patrol?' the countess raised her eyebrows. 'I don't think they had that in 1887.'

'They're bird agents,' Tiny Tony explained. 'They go round helping poultry defeat their enemies. In this case that means you, Countess. Sounds like you had a lucky escape, no thanks to your pal Thaddeus here.' He turned to Thaddeus. 'Satisfied now, Fox? Turns out you were wrong about everything. Rooster sent his chicken squad *and* James Pond to protect the Fogsham Farm roost.'

'Good,' Thaddeus E. Fox said. A brilliantly evil plot was forming in his mind. It was *so* brilliantly evil, it was his turn to be smug. Pond was from Poultry Patrol. He could lead them to Rooster. It was just a simple matter of persuading him to help . . .

'GOOD?' Tiny Tony Tiddles spat back. 'How is it good? You've screwed up, Fox. You promised us chicken and now we've got another fight with Rooster and co on our paws. I wanna know what you're gonna do about it!'

Thaddeus turned his cunning yellow eyes on the cat. It was time to show Tiny Tony who was boss. 'I'll fix Pond,' he said. 'And the chickens, *and* Professor Rooster.' He paused, then added menacingly, 'And if you don't back down, Tiddles, I'll fix you too.' He eyed Tiny Tony coldly. 'I've always wanted a black and white fur hat to go with my red coat.'

Tiny Tony gulped. 'Okay, okay,' he said. 'Keep your brush on.'

Thaddeus beckoned the Pigeon-Poo Gang down from the ledge. They fluttered reluctantly to the table.

'Pond's injured,' he said. 'Find out where the chickens are keeping him at the farm.'

'What about our grain?' the leader of the Pigeon-Poo Gang demanded.

'Tomorrow,' Thaddeus said firmly. 'I promise.' He opened the door of the dungeon for the Pigeon-Poo Gang. The pigeons sidled out and flew away along the corridor.

There was a horrible squawking from outside.

'Leave them alone, Ichabod!' the countess shouted. 'I've told you before, the poo pigeons are our guests!'

'Yes, m'lady,' Ichabod's voice echoed back.

The squawking got louder.

'And that goes for you too, Granny Wishbone!'

'Yeeeesssss, m'laaadyyyyyy!' Granny Wishbone's terrible screech had all four remaining villains holding their paws over their ears.

'She's really feisty, that one!' the countess said when the squawking stopped. She wrinkled her snout. 'Not much blood, though. Very scrawny.'

Thaddeus E. Fox leaned forward. 'I congratulate you on your excellent taste in zombies, Countess,' he

said. 'With your permission I propose to use them in my brilliantly evil plan.'

'Of course, darling,' the countess agreed, 'although I have to warn you Ichabod is rather gooey. Does that matter?'

'Not at all,' Thaddeus smirked. 'The gooier the better.' He outlined his idea.

'That's horrible, darling!' the countess commended him. 'How clever of you!'

''Orrible but ingenious!' Kebab Claude agreed.

'Yeah, not bad,' Tiny Tony Tiddles said grudgingly, 'for you.'

'Thank you,' Thaddeus said. He banged his stick on the table. 'This time tomorrow, ladies and gentlemen, we shall be feasting on fowl,' he boasted, 'with a generous serving of rooster blood: *Professor Rooster* blood, to be precise. Now get me Granny Wishbone. I have a job for her and Ichabod.'

Chapter Eleven

That same evening at Fogsham Farm, Amy, Boo and Ruth were in the leisure centre shed saying goodnight to James Pond.

Amy regarded the duck without sympathy. Apart from the fact that his head was still bandaged he looked fine to her. He was certainly eating plenty. She and Ruth and Boo had been running about all day getting him snacks and drinks. That was when they weren't banging nails into the chicken sheds. Amy felt exhausted. It was hard work being a chicken warrior, especially with James Pond bossing you around all the time.

The three chickens hung about while Rossiter Brown took James Pond's pulse. It was Rossiter Brown's idea that the leisure centre shed should act as a temporary hospital. At the moment the only patient was James Pond, but Amy was secretly worried that Rossiter thought there might be more casualties before their mission was over.

'How are you feeling now?' Rossiter asked.

'Not too bad,' James Pond replied. 'I've just got a bit of a headache. I'll be fine in the morning.'

'There's nothing wrong with him!' Amy muttered to her friends. 'He's putting it on to get attention.'

'We don't *know* he's putting it on, Amy,' Ruth

reasoned. 'Head injuries can be very nasty. And Pond's had two from the same Zimmer frame in the past twelve hours. That can't be good.'

'I'm telling you, he is!' Amy argued back. 'He should be out there slaying Fangula, not lying about in bed!'

'Well, there's nothing we can do about it now,' Boo sighed. 'Rossiter won't let him out until tomorrow morning. And anyway, it's too late to slay Fangula. It got dark ages ago.'

Amy glanced at the shed window. Boo was right. She'd barely noticed but the day had slipped past. Fangula was probably already out of her coffin prowling around somewhere on the moor with Granny Wishbone and Ichabod Comb. There was no choice but to wait.

'We'd better get going,' Rossiter said, 'before the humans turn off their lights.' He gave James Pond some green leaves to chew. 'Eat these. They're herbs. They'll help with the headache. Don't be too long,' he told the chickens, letting himself out of the shed.

'We won't,' Amy promised.

James Pond munched the herbs and lay back on his straw bed. 'Did you check all the sheds for holes?' he asked.

'Yes,' said Amy wearily. 'We've checked the walls and the windows and the doors. They're all fine.'

'Okay, then,' James Pond yawned, 'you hens hit the hay. Make sure you nail up the door when you leave.'

The chickens said goodnight and filed out of the shed. Amy was glad of the faint light coming from the farmhouse. It should keep Fangula away for the time being.

'What's that noise?' Boo asked nervously.

Amy listened hard. 'It sounds like pigs,' she said.

'It's the granny chickens,' said Ruth. 'They're snoring again.'

'At least we don't have to listen to *them* tonight!' Amy said. She was looking forward to snuggling down with the other chickens in the sleeping coop. She thought she might plug her ears with straw to make sure she got a good night's sleep.

'Have you got the hammer and nails, Ruth?' Boo asked.

'Check.' Ruth removed them from the Emergency Chicken Pack.

'I'll do it,' Amy volunteered. She took the hammer and bashed in three nails as hard as she could. It was the sort of thing she was used to doing at Perrin's Farm before she became a chicken warrior. The coops there always needed repairing. 'That should hold Fangula and her zombies.' She threw her shoulder against the door. It didn't budge. She stepped back, satisfied. 'Nothing can get in there tonight.' She grinned. 'Or out!' She gave a whoop of joy. 'Which means we can forget Pond for a while and go and have some fun with the other chickens!'

'Hooray!' Boo and Ruth cheered.

'Can we play Twister?' Boo asked.

'No,' said Amy, 'you always win that. And there isn't room. Let's play wing wrestling.'

'But you always win that!' Boo said.

'What about chess?' Ruth suggested.

'Boring!' Boo and Amy said together.

The three chickens scuttled off to the sleeping coop. They were so busy arguing happily about what

111

game they were going to play that they didn't see the three members of the Pigeon-Poo Gang perched on the window ledge of the farm, watching them.

Thaddeus E. Fox waited until the Pigeon-Poo Gang returned from their watch. He sat patiently while their leader traced out a map on the floor of the dungeon with his claw.

'Pond's in the hospital shed,' the pigeon told Thaddeus. 'The chickens are in the sleeping coop with Rossiter and the Fogsham hens.'

'What about the grannies?' Thaddeus asked. Granny Wishbone had told him about her cronies and their outing to the Chicken Zimmer Frame Throwing Championships. The grannies now formed an important part of his brilliantly evil plan.

'In the juice shack, asleep.'

'Good work,' Thaddeus said. It was time to put his plan into action. 'Get Wishbone and Ichabod ready,' he told Kebab Claude. He took his fob watch off and

placed it on the table. 'Bring them to the farm in two hours. I'll be waiting by the wall.' He turned to the countess. 'Do you have any writing paper?' he asked.

'Of course, darling! It's in the kitchen.' The countess led the way along the corridor and pushed open another door.

Thaddeus looked round the kitchen carefully. Once Kebab Claude got the fire going in the grate, Thaddeus decided, it would do very well for the feast. They could keep the prisoners in the dungeon until they were ready to eat them.

'Here we are!' A thick oak table rested in the middle of the kitchen floor. It was covered with Ichabod's various cooking ingredients including bat wings, dried mice and what looked very much like hedgehog brains. The countess swept them onto the floor. She produced a thick cream piece of paper, a quill pen and an ancient bottle of ink from a drawer.

'Why don't you do it, Countess?' Thaddeus suggested. 'As you have such beautiful handwriting?'

'Very well,' the countess dipped the pen in the bottle of ink. 'Tell me what to put.'

Thaddeus murmured his instructions. When the countess had finished writing he waited until he was sure the ink was dry, rolled up the piece of paper, removed the top of his silver cane and slid the scroll into the hollow tube inside. Then he picked up the cane and made his way silently out of the kitchen to the steps of Bloodsucker Hall. He raced through the grounds, under the gate and across the moor until he reached the dry stone wall that surrounded Fogsham Farm. Choosing a spot closest to the chicken sheds, there, very quietly, he began to dig.

Chapter Twelve

SCRATCH! SCRATCH! SCRATCH!

Inside the hospital shed James Pond woke with a start. His eyes went to the door. It was still firmly closed.

SCRATCH! SCRATCH! SCRATCH!

He listened carefully. The scratching was coming from beneath his bed. Something was trying to get in through the floor.

BOOMPH!

James Pond felt himself being catapulted through the air. He landed beak first on the hard floor of the shed. He raised his head groggily.

'Time for your medicine, Mr Pond,' a voice screeched.

James Pond sat up. It must be another one of the hens from the sleeping coop, come to check up on him, he thought. Funny that Rossiter hadn't mentioned that they had a system of tunnels under the sheds. Quite clever for chickens, he decided. They were usually as

dim as dodos. 'I've already had my medicine,' he said. 'Rossiter gave it to me.'

'All right, your bath, then,' came the voice.

'I don't want a bath!' James Pond said crossly. 'I want to go to sleep.'

'Doctor's orders!' the voice insisted.

'What doctor?' James Pond said. Rossiter hadn't said anything about a doctor.

'Doctor Ichabod,' screeched the voice.

'Look, what is this?' James Pond reached for a torch. He switched it on. The beam of light swept the shed floor. He could see a raised floorboard where the hen had entered. The hen was standing beside it. James Pond pulled a face. Her feet were covered in knobbly corns.

'Oh no you don't!' the voice yelled.

The feet set off at a brisk trot towards him. James Pond felt the torch being knocked out of his wing. 'Ouch!' he exclaimed. The beam of light shone uselessly into the corner of the shed.

'Doctor Ichabod doesn't like too much light when he operates,' the hen continued. 'Do you, Doctor?'

 117

'No,' a second voice grunted.

'Operates!' James Pond repeated. 'What are you talking about? I'm fine.'

'You are now,' the hen rasped. 'But you won't be when Doctor Ichabod has finished with you.'

James Pond felt frantically for the torch. His outstretched wing made contact with the handle. He managed to swing it round so that the light illuminated the shed. He blinked. Two figures loomed over him. He recognised one of them from the fight at The Bloodless Hen. Only she looked different from the last time he'd seen her. More ugly and wizened, if that were possible, and more like she'd just died from the bubonic plague.

'Granny Wishbone!' James Pond gasped.

Granny Wishbone was covered in boils. Her milky eyes were crazed with red, like raspberry ripple ice cream. She had fang marks on the side of her neck. 'That's right, Pond!' she cackled. 'Meet my new friend, Ichabod.'

'Hello.' Ichabod Comb stepped forwards. He had a doctor's coat on. A stethoscope swung from his neck. Goo dripped from the end.

'Hold it right there!' James Pond ordered. He reached for Vladimir's Vampire Slayer. 'Or I'll shoot.'

'Be our guests!' Granny Wishbone chortled.

PHUT!

The pencil hit Granny Wishbone in the eye. She pulled it out. James Pond gasped. Her eyeball was on the end of it!

Granny Wishbone plucked the eyeball off and stuck it back in the socket. 'Ha ha, you missed!' she

screeched. 'Anyway, you can't kill *us* with that, only the countess!' she swiped the holder out of James Pond's wing. 'And she's at Bloodsucker Hall preparing for a feast with her new friends.'

'What new friends?'

'A very posh gentleman fox,' said Granny Wishbone, counting them off on her fingers, 'a smelly poodle, a cat in a hat and some tasty-looking pigeons.'

'The MOST WANTED Club!' James Pond gasped. 'You'll never get away with this!'

'Yes, we will,' said Granny Wishbone. 'Seize him, Ichabod!'

'Yes, ma'am!' Ichabod Comb raised his mangy wings and grabbed James Pond by the feet.

James Pond kicked out at him. 'Let me go!'

A few more of Ichabod's feathers fell off. 'Shan't.' Ichabod Comb held him fast while Granny Wishbone tied a bandage round James Pond's ankles.

'What do you want?' James Pond struggled frantically.

'Information,' Granny Wishbone said. 'Where's Professor Rooster?'

'I don't know!' James Pond said. 'And even if I did I wouldn't tell you.'

Ichabod Comb tied his ankles to the door handle. He grabbed James Pond by the throat.

'We can do this the easy way, or the hard way,' Granny Wishbone screeched. 'Either you quack or Ichabod goos you.' She pulled the stethoscope towards James Pond's beak. A drop of goo quivered on the end. It dropped with a soft plop on James Pond's bow tie.

'No!' James Pond twisted away. 'You won't get anything from me!'

'Hmm,' Granny Wishbone's eyes narrowed. 'You're harder to crack than a hen's tooth. Which gives me an idea!' She leaned towards him and removed her false teeth.

'What are you doing?' James Pond struggled.

'The bite of a vampire is swift,' Granny Wishbone said. 'But being gummed to death by a zombie chicken is something else altogether.'

Her gums closed around his throat.

'Noooooo!' James Pond screamed. 'I'll tell you anything. Just get off me!'

 121

Granny Wishbone sat back. She put her teeth back in. 'So,' she said in a soft voice, 'keep quacking, duck. Where's Rooster?'

At his top-secret location somewhere on the Dudley Estate, Professor Rooster sat at his desk surrounded by a mountain of work. He couldn't concentrate on any of it. He was worried. It was two days since he'd heard from his elite chicken squad and there was no word from Rossiter Brown either. The Professor switched on his laptop and tried again to reach Chicken HQ. He had been trying all day, but with no joy. There had been no reply from Amy, Boo or Ruth.

The screen fizzled into life. He tapped at some keys. Chicken HQ came into view. The professor could see the inside of the three potting sheds with the chickens' beds at one end and the gadgets cupboard at the other. But there was no sign of the chickens.

Amy, Boo and Ruth had still not returned from Fogsham Farm.

He sighed. Perhaps it had been a mistake to send them on the vampire mission. They were very young. And they had only ever completed one mission before. Perhaps he should have got help from Poultry Patrol: James Pond, for instance. Pond was one of the best agents he knew. He was one of the very few birds the Professor trusted to keep a secret. Professor Rooster's wings hovered over the laptop. Then he typed in a secret code and spoke into the microphone.

'This is Professor Rooster,' he said. 'Is that Poultry Patrol?'

'Yes,' a voice came back, 'can I help?'

'Is Pond available?' the professor asked. 'I need him at once.'

'Pond?' the operator sounded surprised. 'But he's already booked out on a mission under your name.'

'What?' Professor Rooster frowned. 'But I don't understand.'

'He called in a couple of days ago,' the operator told him, 'to say he was delayed. He said he'd agreed to help your hens with a secret mission: something about a vampire mink . . . I assumed you knew.'

'I see . . .' Professor Rooster's face was grim. 'Thank you.' He ended the call.

Pond was helping his elite chicken squad already? Professor Rooster felt betrayed. The chickens hadn't said anything about getting James Pond to help them. And Pond hadn't told him either.

Professor Rooster got ready for bed. He brushed his teeth and preened his feathers half-heartedly. He massaged his bad leg – still sore from when

Thaddeus E. Fox had once caught him in his powerful jaws – and lay down on his straw pallet. Tomorrow he would find out from his bird spies what was going on at Bleakley Fogsham. And then he would do some serious thinking. He needed a team he could trust. And if that meant getting a new elite combat squad and sending Amy, Boo and Ruth home, he would do it. He was fond of them, of course, and they had done their best. He was glad they had managed to defeat Fox and his gang, at least. But if he couldn't trust them, they would have to go. He closed his eyes.

Just then the door flew open.

Professor Rooster sat up with a start. Standing before him was a small black and white cat and a large French poodle.

'Tiddles!' the Professor gasped. 'Claude! But how did you . . . ?'

'Pond quacked,' Tiny Tony Tiddles said shortly. 'He told us where your secret hideout was. Your old pal Thaddeus sent me and Claude to chicken-nap you. Claude, give me the sack.'

Kebab Claude was helping himself to a drink of

water from the professor's water trough. He shook the drool from his mouth and untied the sack from around his neck. "Ere you are,' he said.

Tiny Tony Tiddles opened it. 'The Countess von Fangula is waiting for you at Bloodsucker Hall, Professor Rooster,' he purred. 'She's getting kinda thirsty for rooster blood.'

The professor drew himself up to his full height. He was taller than Tiny Tony. 'What if I refuse to go with you?' he said.

'That ain't an option, Professor,' Tiny Tony held his ground. 'Hold him, Claude.'

Professor Rooster felt two hefty paws clasp his wings from behind. He tried to struggle, but it was hopeless. He felt himself being bundled into the sack and borne away into the darkness.

Chapter Thirteen

'Cock-a-doodle-doooooooooooooooo!'

'I wish Rossiter wouldn't make such a racket!' Amy complained.

It was morning at Fogsham Farm. Rossiter Brown had gone outside to wake up the humans and remind them to leave the chickens some grain. He was crowing loudly.

'Maybe we shouldn't have stayed up so late playing games,' Ruth yawned. 'We slept in.'

'You've got to admit it was fun, though,' Amy said. Because they couldn't agree which game to play, in the end the chickens had played *all* the games they could think of. They'd even made room for Twister, which the chicks enjoyed.

'How come everyone else is still asleep?' Boo said blearily.

All the other hens were still slumbering peacefully in the hay.

'They're used to it, I suppose,' Amy said. She pulled a few strands of hay out of her ears: Rossiter's crowing was so loud her earplugs didn't seem to make any difference. She got up and stretched. It was quite cramped in the sleeping coop. She needed to stretch her legs. And they still had a mission to complete. Or, at least, James Pond did. 'Let's go and wake up old lazy-bones,' she said. 'Fangula will be back in her coffin by now.'

'Oh,' said Boo. Her face clouded. 'I'd forgotten all about the mission. I had such a nice time last night.' She jumped up. 'But you're right, Amy. We should get going. The professor's relying on us.'

Boo's words made Amy feel guilty. For the first time it dawned on her why it had been wrong not to tell Professor Rooster about James Pond. It wasn't for the reason she'd thought – that the professor would find out they needed help to complete the mission. It was because although not telling the professor wasn't exactly a lie, it wasn't exactly the truth either. Boo was right. The professor *was* relying on them. And if he couldn't rely on them to tell him the truth, he couldn't rely on them for anything.

'What's the matter, Amy?' Ruth asked. 'You look fed up.'

'Nothing,' Amy lied. It had been her idea to keep it a secret. What if the professor found out? What if he was cross? It wasn't just her who would get into trouble: Boo and Ruth would too. Amy felt all muddled and upset. She needed to do some chicken thinking.

The three chickens let themselves out of the sleeping coop. Rossiter was just coming to the end of his song. Amy heard the clank of pails being emptied and the pad-pad-pad of rubber boots retreating to the farmhouse.

'It's okay,' Rossiter said. 'The humans have gone. I'll go and check on the grannies, then I'll be back.' He strutted off.

Amy trailed after the others across the farmyard to the hospital shed. Ruth had brought the Emergency Chicken Pack. She took out the hammer and squinted at the nails.

'I'll do it,' Amy said. She tucked the claw of the hammer behind the head of the first nail and levered

129

it out. Doing something practical made her feel better. She resolved that she would do everything possible to help James Pond complete the mission. And after that she would tell the professor the truth – that it was her idea to get James Pond to do the dirty work and to keep it a secret from him – at least then the professor couldn't blame Boo and Ruth.

PLINK! PLINK! PLINK!

The three nails dropped on the floor one after the other. 'You can open the door now,' Amy said. She bent down to pick up the nails. She heard the door creak, then a gasp. 'What is it?' Amy looked up in alarm.

'He's gone!' Boo said.

Amy crowded into the shed behind Boo and Ruth. She looked round in horror. The floor had been ripped up. A few duck feathers lay strewn on the hay. Vladimir's Vampire Slayer and a torch had been kicked into a corner. A trail of something sticky led across the floor. 'Someone must have tunnelled into the hospital shed while we were asleep,' she said.

'Fangula!' Boo whispered.

'Not necessarily,' Ruth said in her serious voice.

She put a magnifying glass to her eye and examined the floor.

'Where did you get that from?' Amy asked in awe. Ruth looked like a super-brainy detective!

'The Emergency Chicken Pack,' Ruth replied. 'Professor Rooster must have thought it would come in useful.'

'Oh.' Amy couldn't bear to think about Professor Rooster. What on earth would he say when he found out James Pond had disappeared? A dreadful thought

occurred to her. *What if James Pond had been turned into a zombie?*

'What do you mean it's not necessarily Fangula?' Boo asked Ruth.

'This is zombie goo,' Ruth said, pointing at the sticky trail, 'not blood. That means Pond was snatched by Ichabod and Granny Wishbone, not by Fangula herself.'

'Does it matter?' Amy asked dismally.

'It might,' said Ruth. She moved towards the hole in the floor. 'Hmmm, another clue,' she said, unthreading a piece of orange fluff from one of the splintered floorboards and examining it carefully with the magnifying glass. 'Whatever it was that tunnelled underneath the shed left this behind.'

'What is it?' asked Boo.

'Take a look.' Ruth said.

Boo took the magnifying glass. 'Flap!' she exclaimed. 'Amy, you'd better look at this.'

'All right.' Amy peered through the thick glass at the orange fluff. She blinked. It wasn't fluff at all. It was a tuft of orange fur.

The three chickens stared at one another.

'Are you thinking what I'm thinking?' Ruth asked eventually.

'I think so,' Boo replied.

The two chickens looked expectantly at Amy.

'I think I think I'm thinking it!' Amy said. She waited. She didn't want to be the one who said what it was they were all supposed to be thinking in case she'd got it wrong!

'This fur belongs to a fox: Thaddeus E. Fox, if I'm not very much mistaken,' Ruth said finally.

'Are you sure?' Amy asked in a small voice. She didn't know whether to be pleased or disappointed that she'd guessed right.

'It's the only logical explanation,' Ruth replied. 'Professor Rooster told us that there were no foxes on the moor in winter. He said they went to ground. So we know it's no ordinary fox we're dealing with here. That leaves Thaddeus.'

Amy felt worse than ever. *Fangula and Thaddeus E. Fox! Even James Pond won't stand a chance against those two!* Suddenly she burst into tears.

'Amy, what's wrong?' Boo put her wing round her.

'This is all my fault!' Amy howled. 'I wish I'd never asked James Pond to help us. I wish I'd told the professor the truth. He's going to be so cross with me when he finds out what's happened.'

'It's not your fault, Amy,' Boo said firmly. 'We agreed to it, didn't we, Ruth?'

Ruth nodded. 'Of course we did. It was all of us, Amy, not just you. None of us wanted to slay Fangula. That's why we asked James Pond to do it.'

'But you were going to tell the professor,' Amy sniffed. 'It was me who said we shouldn't.'

'We didn't tell him, though, did we?' Boo pointed out. 'We went along with it. Which makes us just as much to blame for what's happened as you.'

'Really?' Amy smiled tearfully. She was so lucky to have such good friends.

'Really.' Boo and Ruth gave her a hug.

'Anyway, Amy,' Ruth added, 'it's not *your* fault Thaddeus E. Fox decided to put in an appearance. None of us were expecting that.'

That was true, Amy thought. Professor Rooster couldn't blame her for Thaddeus showing up.

Ruth took off her specs and polished them with her scarf. She had that brainy detective look on her face again, Amy noticed. She decided to forget about her own problems for a minute and concentrate.

'The question is, why did Thaddeus get the zombies to snatch James Pond?' Ruth said thoughtfully. 'Why didn't he and Fangula just eat him when they had the chance?'

'You think James Pond is still alive?' Amy cried, her heart filling with hope.

'I reckon there's a good chance that he is,' Ruth said. 'Fox planned this specially. I mean why go after James Pond at all? Why didn't the villains just raid the sleeping coop?'

'Maybe Thaddeus got the wrong shed?' Boo suggested.

Ruth shook her head. 'Thaddeus won't be here alone,' she said. 'The rest of the MOST WANTED Club will be in on the plan too. My guess is Thaddeus would have got the Pigeon-Poo Gang to check out

the lie of the land before he started digging so he didn't get the sheds mixed up.'

'Maybe he was frightened *we'd* be waiting for him?' Amy said. 'Fangula must have told him we rescued James Pond from her coffin yesterday.'

'I don't think it's that either,' Ruth replied. 'We didn't even know Fox and his gang were here. He could have taken us by surprise.' She scratched her head. 'He chose the hospital shed deliberately. He wanted Pond and he wanted him alive. I'm sure of it. I just don't get why!'

Amy thought hard. 'Know your enemy,' she said suddenly. It was something the chickens had learned when they had been training to become chicken warriors.

'Amy's right,' Boo said. 'We've got to get inside his head. We've got to think like foxes.'

The three chickens screwed their eyes tight shut.

Amy tried to imagine she was Thaddeus E. Fox. *What could be so important to him that he would sacrifice raiding a chicken shed – killing the three of them, even! – to snatch James Pond instead?* Pond must have something Thaddeus E. Fox wanted more than anything else in the world.

There was only one thing she could think of . . .

Amy's eyes flew open. 'Professor Rooster!' she cried. 'That's why Thaddeus E. Fox wanted James Pond alive: he's the only one of us who knows where the professor lives.'

Boo and Ruth stared at her, shocked.

'Pond won't tell him, though,' Boo whispered. 'Will he?'

'He might not tell Thaddeus,' Amy said grimly, 'but I don't think even James Pond could stand up to Granny Wishbone, especially now she's a zombie.'

'So that was Fox's plan all along!' Ruth said. 'To find out from Pond where the professor lives and chicken-nap him!'

Just then Rossiter Brown appeared in the doorway holding a scroll of paper. His face was grave.

Now what? thought Amy.

'It's the grannies,' Rossiter said, 'they're not in the juice shed.'

Chapter Fourteen

'I found this.' Rossiter Brown held out the paper.

Ruth took it. She uncurled the scroll and began to read.

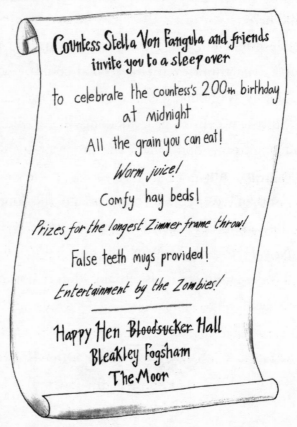

Countess Stella Von Fangula and friends invite you to a sleepover

to celebrate the countess's 200th birthday at midnight

All the grain you can eat!

Warm juice!

Comfy hay beds!

Prizes for the longest Zimmer frame throw!

False teeth mugs provided!

Entertainment by the Zombies!

Happy Hen ~~Bloodsucker~~ Hall
Bleakley Fogsham
The Moor

'Flap!' said Amy. 'You mean the grannies fell for that?'

'I fear they must have,' Rossiter Brown replied. 'I think they sneaked out when the rest of us were asleep.'

'That means Fangula will have turned them into zombies by now!' Boo wailed.

Amy shivered. Fangula's zombie army was back. Only this time it was made up of Granny Wishbone and her cronies. The idea was horrible: the grannies were bad enough even when they weren't zombies. She dreaded the thought of what they would be like now. 'How did they get out?' she asked, although she thought she already knew the answer.

'Through a tunnel,' Rossiter said. 'It goes under the shed through the farmyard to the other side of the dry stone wall, where the path to Bloodsucker Hall begins.' He shook his head sadly. 'I didn't know Fangula could dig.'

'Fangula didn't dig the tunnel,' Amy told him. 'It was Thaddeus E. Fox. He and his MOST WANTED Club of villains have teamed up with the countess. James Pond has disappeared as well.'

She filled him in on their news as quickly as she could.

'The professor!' Rossiter gasped when she got to the bit about Professor Rooster being chicken-napped.

'I'm afraid so,' Boo said solemnly. She put a wing round his shoulder to comfort him.

'But what are we going to do now?' Rossiter flapped. 'I mean it's only a matter of time before the villains attack the sleeping coop.' He put his head in his wings. 'We're finished.'

'No we're not,' Amy tried to sound brave. 'We'll rescue the professor. He'll know what to do.'

'What if you're too late?' Rossiter said. 'What if Fangula has already turned him into a zombie?'

Amy's face fell. She hadn't thought of that.

'We won't be too late,' Ruth said.

'How do you know?' asked Rossiter.

'Maths.'

'Maths?' Amy echoed.

'Yes. What time did we go to bed last night, Boo?'

'About nine o'clock, I think.'

Ruth took out the pencil from the Emergency

Chicken Pack and jotted down some numbers on the back of the invitation. 'Let's say Thaddeus waited an hour after we went to bed before he started digging . . . and it took him another hour to dig the first tunnel and deliver the invitation to the juice shed . . .' She scribbled something on the paper '. . . that means the grannies must have escaped at about eleven o'clock last night.'

Amy listened carefully. She'd never been much good at maths, or telling the time, for that matter. It was a good thing Ruth was so good at numbers.

'Then he had to dig a *second* tunnel to the hospital shed and send Ichabod and Granny Wishbone down it to get James Pond and make him quack. That would take us to, say . . .' Ruth chewed the pencil, '. . . midnight!' She scribbled more numbers down. '*Then* one of the MOST WANTED Club had to run twenty miles across country to fetch the professor . . .'

'That would take ages if you didn't have flight-booster engines,' Amy remarked.

'Exactly my point,' Ruth beamed at her. 'By the time whoever it was made it back to Bloodsucker Hall with the professor . . .'

'. . . it would be dawn!' Boo exclaimed.

'And Fangula would be back in her coffin!' Amy cried. She got it now. Of course the professor was still alive. Fangula and her zombies only operated in darkness. And it had taken the villains until dawn to chicken-nap Professor Rooster. 'Oh, Ruth, you are clever!' she sighed.

'Thanks!' Ruth blushed.

'So you've got until sunset to rescue the professor and save the roost,' Rossiter Brown said, sounding more cheerful.

'How long is that?' Boo asked.

'About four hours,' said Ruth.

Four hours! Amy wished it didn't get dark so early on the moor and that they hadn't slept in. Four hours didn't seem a very long time to do all those difficult things. But it would just have to do. 'That should be plenty,' she said brightly, crossing her tail feathers behind her bottom so that Rossiter Brown couldn't see.

'I'll go and tell the others.' Rossiter Brown hurried out of the hospital shed.

'Er . . . just one small problem, Amy,' Boo said. 'How are we going to get the professor out of Bloodsucker Hall without Thaddeus and his gang catching us?'

'I don't know,' Amy admitted. 'Maybe we should have a look in the Emergency Chicken Pack and see if there's anything in there we can use.'

Ruth emptied out the contents onto the floor of the shed.

The magnifying glass fell out, followed by the Mite Blaster Grease squirt, the hammer, the pencil sharpener and a spare garlic tube for the garlic blaster.

'Is that it?' Amy asked, disappointed.

'No, there's something else.' Ruth gave the pack another shake.

A short round cylinder with holes in one end rolled along the floor, leaving a trail of black powder behind it.

'Aaaaaaa-shoo!' Amy sneezed.

Ruth picked up the cylinder. 'It's a pepper shaker,' she said.

'What's it for,' asked Amy, 'apart from to make you sneeze?'

 143

'That's exactly what it's for' said Ruth. 'Animals don't like pepper. Humans use it to keep them off their land. I think it's meant to be a weapon.'

That was useful, thought Amy. She stored the information away in her little chicken brain. 'Anything else?' she asked.

Ruth gave the bag a final jiggle.

CLANG! A flat square tin tumbled out onto the floor.

Amy picked it up and examined it. The tin had writing on the side.

'What's that for?' asked Ruth, baffled for once.

'A disguise!' Amy said gleefully. She'd once been to a Halloween party at Perrin's Farm where all the chickens had dressed up in different scary costumes and gone round the barn asking for sweetcorn from the other farm animals.

'How does that help us?' Boo asked.

Amy smiled happily. She might not be much good at maths but she'd just had one of her occasional flashes of chicken genius. 'We'll use it to get past Thaddeus E. Fox and the MOST WANTED Club, of course!' She flipped open the tin lid. Three sets of yellow rubber teeth grinned back at her. She picked up a sponge and dabbed it in green make-up. 'Now, who wants to be first?' she said.

Chapter Fifteen

Down in the kitchen at Bloodsucker Hall, Thaddeus E. Fox sat in a moth-eaten armchair with his back paws in a bowl of hot soapy water. It had been hard work digging the tunnels to the chicken sheds and his feet were sore. But it had been worth it. His plan had worked perfectly. He had captured Pond. He had captured Rooster. The countess had an army of granny chicken zombies. And there was nothing that Professor Rooster's pesky chicken squad could do about it. Thaddeus E. Fox let out a contented sigh.

One last raid on the sleeping coop at Fogsham Farm tonight and they would finally be ready for the banquet to begin.

'How's the barbecue, Claude?' he asked.

Kebab Claude was bending over the fireplace with a pair of iron tongs. 'Nice and 'ot,' he said, turning over the burning logs.

'What about the carving knives?' Thaddeus said. 'Are they sharp?'

'Sharp as my own claws,' Tiny Tony Tiddles looked up from beside the fire. A silver carving set lay beside him, glinting in a box on a bed of faded blue velvet.

'Excellent.' Thaddeus E. Fox felt so relaxed he was even prepared to be nice to Tiny Tony. The cat and the poodle had done well last night, he thought, carrying Rooster all that way across country in a sack. The professor was big and surprisingly heavy for a bird. It had taken three of them to clap the cockerel in irons when Kebab Claude and Tiny Tony Tiddles finally made it back to the hall at daybreak. Rooster had struggled and flapped. Thaddeus had been tempted to bash him over the head with his silver cane and eat him there and then. He was glad that he had been patient, though. What a pleasure it would be to see his good friend, the countess, sink her fangs into Professor Rooster's neck while he, Thaddeus, tucked into James Pond and the three members of the professor's elite chicken squad for his hors d'oeuvre. It was he, Thaddeus E. Fox, who would have the last laugh. PHWA HA HA HA HA!

Kebab Claude had prepared a menu. Thaddeus read it again.

Starter

Chicken

Main Course

More Chicken

Pudding

Duck

Vampire option

(Professor) Rooster blood

'Has anyone checked on the prisoners recently?' he asked.

'I did,' the leader of the Pigeon-Poo Gang replied. 'They're as snug as a slug in my mug.'

'Good work.' Thaddeus E. Fox was glad the pigeons were keeping a close watch. Not that there was any possibility of the prisoners escaping, he thought, but it was just possible that Rooster's chickens might work out what was happening and come looking for him. One of them was clever – the tall one with the glasses. The others were just plain dumb, especially the little fat one with the wrestling moves. Thaddeus curled his lip. *Let them come*, he thought. They wouldn't get the better of him again, that was for sure.

Just then he heard a noise in the corridor outside. He pricked up his ears.

PITTER PATTER PITTER PATTER.

It was the sound of running feet. *Chicken* feet, if he wasn't very much mistaken. Maybe it was Professor Rooster's squad! His eyes gleamed at the thought. He fancied a little snack before dinner.

Thaddeus E. Fox got out of his chair and dried

his paws on the rug. Putting his finger to his lips to warn the other villains to be quiet he padded to the kitchen door and threw it open.

He jumped.

The sight that met his eyes was vile. Three members of the countess's new zombie army stood before him. One was tall with glasses and a scarf, one was medium sized with feathery boots and a backpack, and one was small and plump with red cheeks. All of them had rotten teeth. Their eyeballs dangled down their cheeks. Boils erupted from between their green feathers and their toes were covered in corns.

Thaddeus E. Fox couldn't decide which was worse: the goo dripping from their noses, the horrible scar tattoos on their legs or the blood gushing from their mouths. He had never seen anything so disgusting in his life.

'What are you doing here?' he asked.

The zombie chickens looked at one another. 'The countess sent us,' the small one shrieked.

Thaddeus put his paws to his ears.

'What for?' he demanded.

'To check on the prisoners,' the zombie chicken screamed.

'We've just done that,' Thaddeus E. Fox grumbled. 'Go back and tell the countess they're fine.'

The zombies didn't budge.

'I said, push off,' Thaddeus growled. The sight of the three chickens was making him feel sick. He hoped they weren't planning to come to the feast. It would put him off his food. 'Well, what are you waiting for?'

The three chickens looked at one another.

'Garlic,' the tall one grunted.

'What about it?' asked Thaddeus.

'We need to make sure the rooster hasn't eaten any,' it said.

'Vampire's orders,' groaned the one with feathery boots.

'Oh, all right, then!' Thaddeus couldn't bear to look at them any more. 'Rooster's in the dungeon next door with the duck. Hurry up, though.'

He went back into the kitchen and slammed the door.

'What was all that about?' Tiny Tony Tiddles demanded.

'Nothing,' Thaddeus settled back in his chair and closed his eyes. He decided to forget about the zombies and have a nap. Very soon he was fast asleep.

Amy, Boo and Ruth hurried along the corridor.

'Phew!' Amy hissed. 'That was close. I thought he wasn't going to let us past. Good thinking about the garlic, Ruth!'

'Thanks!'

'Here it is,' Boo said.

They had reached the dungeon. The three chickens pushed at the heavy door with all their might.

CRRRREEEAAAAKKKK!

They tiptoed in.

Inside the dungeon it was very dark. At first Amy couldn't make anything out. Then, as her eyes got used to the gloom, she saw the professor huddled in a corner with James Pond. Professor Rooster was resting his wing against his head. He looked to be deep in thought. James Pond appeared to be asleep. They were both chained to the wall by the ankles.

'Professor Rooster!' Amy squawked.

Professor Rooster looked astonished to see her. Suddenly she felt a bit shy. She'd never actually met Professor Rooster in the flesh before. She'd only ever seen him on the laptop. It was a bit like meeting a film star or a head teacher or some other important grown-up. And she was still worried he might be cross with her. She didn't know what to say.

Boo and Ruth stepped forward.

'Hello, Professor,' said Ruth awkwardly.

'Hello!' said Boo.

Professor Rooster opened his beak to reply when James Pond woke up.

At the sight of the three chickens James Pond recoiled. 'Aaarrrrrrggghgghhhh!' he screamed. He scrambled to his feet, opened his wings and started flapping. 'Go away!' he yelled. 'I've told you everything I know.'

'What's the matter?' Amy said crossly. 'Can't he see we're here to rescue him?'

'I don't think he can, Amy,' said Professor Rooster. 'He thinks you're zombies.'

'Oh,' said Amy. She had forgotten all about their disguise, she was so overawed at meeting the professor.

'Poor James has had rather a rough time of it with Granny Wishbone and Ichabod, I'm afraid.' The professor grasped James Pond's wings. 'It's all right, James,' he said calmly, 'they're not really zombies!'

'They're not?' James Pond stopped flapping.

'No, it's Amy, Boo and Ruth,' the professor explained patiently. 'They didn't mean to frighten you.'

'Yeah, sorry about that,' said Amy.

'I'm glad the Zombie Kit came in useful.' Professor Rooster examined them carefully. 'You look eggsactly like the real thing,' he said approvingly. 'Absolutely hideous; quite revolting, in fact.'

'Thanks!' Amy said.

'Amy did the make-up,' said Boo.

Amy blushed with pride. She felt her cheeks glow red under the green foundation.

'We even scared Thaddeus E. Fox!' Amy said. She told Professor Rooster what had happened.

'Well done, all of you.' The professor nodded. 'We'd better get out of here, before Fox realises he's been tricked.'

James Pond strained at the iron manacles. 'It's no good!' he quacked, collapsing back on the floor. 'We're trapped!'

'No you're not.' Ruth reached into the Emergency Chicken Pack and drew out the Mite Blaster Grease squirt. 'Stay still.' She squirted the grease onto James Pond's ankles. 'Now try,' she said.

James Pond pulled and struggled. 'I can't!' he said.

'I'll help you.' Amy grasped James Pond under the wingpits and heaved. *SCHLOOP! SCHLOOP!* James Pond's big webbed feet shot out of the manacles.

'Would you like some, Professor?' Ruth asked.

'Just a little, please.'

Ruth gave another squirt with the grease canister.

The professor wriggled his toes through the rings.

'Let's go back to the farm and help Rossiter organise the reinforcements before the villains raid the sleeping coop,' Amy hissed. She crept towards the door.

'Huh-hum,' the professor coughed. 'Aren't you forgetting there's something else you have to do first, Amy?'

Amy stopped mid-creep and turned round. The professor hadn't budged. She regarded him blankly. 'What's that?' she asked.

The professor looked her straight in the eye. His voice was steely. 'You have to complete the mission.'

Chapter Sixteen

Outside, in the grounds of Bloodsucker Hall, the three chickens waved goodbye to Professor Rooster and James Pond. The chickens watched as the two birds made their way through the gates and across the fields towards Fogsham Farm. It was they who were going to help Rossiter Brown organise the reinforcements, not Amy, Boo and Ruth.

Amy let out a heavy sigh. 'I knew Professor Rooster would be cross,' she said.

'He didn't actually *say* he was cross,' Ruth said.

'He didn't have to,' Amy said gloomily. Grown-ups were good at making you feel small and silly without actually saying *anything* at all. And right now she felt very small and silly indeed.

'At least he's given us another chance,' Boo said. 'Maybe if we do it right this time he'll forgive us for not telling the truth.'

'Maybe,' said Amy, brightening a little. 'Let's get

it over with then. Did you remember the Vampire Slayer, Ruth?'

Ruth nodded. 'It's in the Emergency Chicken Pack. With the teaspoons.'

Amy peeked out of their hiding place in the long grass. She checked to make sure the Pigeon-Poo Gang weren't watching them. 'All clear,' she said. 'Thaddeus and his fellow villains must still be in the kitchen preparing for the raid on the chicken sheds.'

They scuttled over to the grave and began to dig. After a little while they heard a familiar *DWANG*. Amy brushed away the last of the soil from the coffin.

The three chickens stared down at it.

'I still don't want to do it,' Boo said in a small voice.

'Me neither,' Ruth agreed.

'Neither do I,' Amy admitted. Then she thought back to the fun they'd had the night before. 'But one of us has to,' she whispered, 'otherwise Fangula and the MOST WANTED Club will kill all our friends at Fogsham Farm.' She took a deep breath. 'I'll do it,' she said. 'I'm the one who's supposed to be brave and I'm the one who got us into all this mess. You two go back to the farm and help the professor.'

Boo and Ruth shook their heads.

'No,' Boo said slowly, 'we're a team. We'll all do it.' She smiled weakly. 'Maybe it won't be so bad if we pull the trigger together.'

'And close our eyes,' Ruth said.

Amy's heart swelled with affection for her friends.

'Thanks,' she whispered gratefully. She tried to make her voice sound business-like. 'How long do we have, Ruth?' she asked.

'There's about an hour of daylight left,' Ruth calculated. 'Unless there's another storm, of course.'

The three chickens glanced at the sky. Black clouds were gathering over Bloodsucker Hall.

The weather was always changing on the moor, Amy reflected. One minute it was sunny, the next minute it was dark, wet and windy. And if it got dark Fangula would pop out of her coffin and the zombies would appear out of the mist, just like Ichabod Comb had the day before. Only this time she, Boo and Ruth would be completely outnumbered by the grizzly grannies.

She had an idea. 'Let's make a circle around the coffin with the garlic from the spare blaster tube. That should hold Fangula for a bit if the storm does come.'

'I'll do that,' Boo offered. She uncorked the tube carefully. Then she tiptoed around the grave scattering minced garlic on the ground. The pungent

smell wafted towards Amy's nostrils. She held her nose.

'I'll assemble the Vampire Slayer.' Ruth rummaged about in the Emergency Chicken Pack.

'And I'll open the coffin lid.' Amy jumped down into the grave. She heaved at the heavy lid and pushed it back on its hinges. Inside the coffin, the Countess Stella von Fangula lay as still as marble.

Amy climbed back out of the grave. 'Ready?' she asked Ruth.

'Er, not quite,' Ruth said. She was still feeling about in the Emergency Chicken Pack.

'What's wrong?' asked Amy.

'I can't find the pencil!' Ruth exclaimed. 'I'm sure it's in here somewhere.' She tipped the contents of the pack out onto the ground.

The three chickens searched through the equipment. There was no sign of the pencil.

'Where can it be?' Boo frowned.

Ruth sat back and scratched her head. 'I remember now!' she exclaimed. 'I had it when I was doing those calculations on the back of the invitation. I must have

left it in the hospital shed. Shall I go and get it?'

'There isn't time!' Amy squawked. Just then there was a clap of thunder from overhead. The storm was upon them. The sky went black. Darkness shrouded the moor.

'What is that horrible smell?' The countess's low voice echoed up from the grave. A paw appeared over the side.

'Quick!' said Amy. 'We need to get outside the garlic circle.'

'Are you sure about that?' Boo whispered. From out of the mist came the zombie army, Granny Wishbone at the head.

Amy froze in panic. She tried to think but her head seemed to be full of straw instead of brains. She wondered if a bit of her earplug from last night was still stuck in there somewhere.

'Let's try the pepper!' cried Ruth. 'That might stop them!'

The three chickens scrabbled about on the ground searching for the pepper shaker. Amy's wing touched the round metal cylinder. She grabbed it and drew it

towards her. Her eye caught a glimpse of her reflection in the polished surface. She started. She had completely forgotten for the second time that they were disguised as zombies. She'd got so used to Boo and Ruth looking mangled that she hadn't given it any thought since they escaped from the dungeon. But now when she saw her own hideous reflection Amy had another one of her strokes of chicken genius.

'We're still in disguise!' she cried. 'The zombies will think we're part of the army. And so will Fangula, if we hurry. Quick, Ruth, help me get the stuff back in the Emergency Chicken Pack.'

The chickens fumbled about in the dark.

Fangula's other paw appeared over the grave. 'Is that you, Granny Wishbone?' she said huskily.

'Over here, m'laaadddy!' Granny Wishbone's screech echoed across the moor.

'Grab what you can!' Amy's wing closed around the handle of the magnifying glass.

'I've got the pepper shaker,' Boo cried.

'And I've got the grease squirt!' shouted Ruth.

They jumped outside the circle of garlic. The gooey

grannie chicken zombies were approaching fast. It was amazing what speed they got up with those Zimmer frames, Amy thought.

GRUNT!

GROAN!

MOAN!

'Act like zombies!' Amy hissed.

'Whoooaaaa!' Ruth staggered about.

'Oooaaaaahhhhh!' Boo sighed.

'Eeerrrrggggh!' Amy bumped into Ichabod Comb. A bit of zombie goo dripped off his head onto her beak. She shook it off.

'I'll go in with the pepper,' Boo said, clutching the shaker.

'No, Boo, wait!' Amy protested.

'I'll be fine,' Boo whispered back. 'Don't worry.' She somersaulted over the heads of the zombies. A blast of pepper shot out of the shaker.

'Aa-aa-shoo!' The grannies started sneezing.

Boo did a graceful back flip. A trail of pepper blew behind her like the smoke from an aeroplane.

'Aaaaaa-aaaa-shoooooo! Aaaaaa-aaaa-shoooooo!

Aaaaaa-aaaa-shoooooo!' The zombies sneezed and sneezed.

'Take cover!' Amy shouted.

Globs of zombie goo rained down on Amy and Ruth.

'What's going on?' The countess emerged from the grave. She screwed up her nose. 'Garlic!' she spat.

'We're under attack, m'lady!' Granny Wishbone screeched. 'Help!'

'Give me a minute!' the countess answered tetchily.

She paced about, trying to find a way through the garlic circle.

'It's holding her!' Ruth whispered.

SPLAT.

SPLUT. SPLUT.

SPLAT!

'What's that?' Amy said.

'Rain,' replied Ruth.

SPLAT.

SPLUT. SPLUT.

SPLAT!

The countess had picked a spot in the garlic circle where the water was collecting into a little stream. She put a paw in it and began to wade across.

'Oh no!' Amy watched in horror. 'The rain is washing away the garlic!'

The countess padded towards Amy and Ruth.

'Act like zombies!' Amy urged.

The two chickens lurched to and fro.

The countess came on slowly, never taking her eyes off them.

'It's not working!' Ruth said.

 167

'Keep lurching!'

SPLAT!

A thick drop of rain landed on Amy's cheek. She wiped it away with her wing. Green make-up came with it. Suddenly Amy understood why Fangula wasn't falling for their zombie act.

'It's the rain!' she whispered. 'It's washing off our disguise.'

Just then Boo landed beside them. 'The pepper's all gone,' she said.

'Now what?' Ruth squawked. They were sandwiched between Fangula and the remains of her gruesome army.

'Think, Ruth!' Amy swallowed. 'Is there any other way to kill a vampire apart from with a wooden stake?'

'I believe you can burn them,' Ruth said.

'But how can we do that when it's pouring with rain?' Boo sobbed.

Just then a ray of sun penetrated the thick cloud.

Von Fangula stopped. She held her front paw up to her eyes. 'Aarrrgggghhhh!' she screamed. 'Sunlight!' She staggered backwards.

The sun disappeared behind another cloud. The countess shook her head and crept forward again.

'I know!' Ruth said suddenly. 'Amy, where's the magnifying glass?'

Amy produced it. 'How's that going to help?'

'If the sun comes out again, we can use it to make a fire! The lens concentrates the sun's rays. If we aim it at Fangula she might sizzle up.'

Amy looked at the sky. The clouds were moving rapidly. Any minute now and there would be another shaft of sunlight. The question was, would it be soon enough? Fangula was only metres away from them.

'The three little chickies who visited me last time,' the countess purred. 'How nice of you to come back.' She prepared to pounce.

'You guys run for it,' Amy shouted. She tried to hold up the magnifying glass but her wing was trembling so much she found she couldn't.

'No,' said Boo. 'We'll do it together.'

Amy felt Boo's strong wing close round hers.

The sun peeped through the cloud.

'We've got to get the angle right.' Ruth took hold

169

of the handle as well. With her other wing she sent a squirt of grease in Fangula's direction.

'Darn it!' Fangula slipped and slithered.

'Get ready,' Ruth whispered.

The three chickens held the magnifying glass aloft.

The sun streamed through the clouds. It shone through the glass lens onto the countess.

'Aarrrrggghhhhh!' the countess screamed. 'I'm burning up!'

'Don't look!' Ruth shouted.

'La la la la la!' Amy closed her eyes.

'Do be do be do!' Boo did the same.

'Once twelve is twelve, twice twelve is twenty-four, three twelves are thirty-six . . .' Ruth recited.

TTTTTTTSSSSSSSSSSSSSSSSSSSSSS! BOOM!
There was a horrible smell of burning, then the sound of a small explosion.

Then silence.

Amy opened one eye. There was no sign of Fangula.

She opened the other eye.

'She's gone!' All that remained of the vampire

mink was a small pile of black soot. A wisp of smoke rose from it and disappeared into the air.

'We did it!' Amy cried. She let go of the magnifying glass and threw herself onto her back with her legs in the air.

Boo joined her. So did Ruth.

The three chickens held wings.

Amy examined her legs. The tattoos were falling off. So were the corns. She took a sideways peek at Boo and Ruth and giggled. What with the smudged green make-up and fake blood dripping down them from the rain they looked more hideous than ever!

'Phew,' said Amy, 'that was close.'

'Yeah, sorry about forgetting the pencil,' said Ruth.

'It's fine,' said Boo. 'I think the magnifying glass worked better, anyway.'

Just then a wizened granny face loomed into view above Amy. *Granny Wishbone!* She was still ugly, but she didn't look as if she had the bubonic plague any more. Fangula's power was finally at an end.

'Eeerrrhh,' said Granny Wishbone. 'What happened

to you three? You look like something from a horror film.'

Amy, Boo and Ruth threw back their beaks and laughed.

Then Amy remembered Thaddeus E. Fox. 'Come on,' she said. 'We'd better get back to the farm. Let's round up the grannies.'

Chapter Seventeen

Down in the kitchen in the ruins of Bloodsucker Hall, Thaddeus E. Fox woke up with a start. He thought he'd heard the countess scream.

TTTTTTTSSSSSSSSSSSSSSSSSSSS! BOOM!

He pricked up his ears. Something outside sizzled, then exploded. It sounded like one of Kebab Claude's sausages had been left on the grill a bit too long.

'What's going on out there?' Tiny Tony Tiddles lifted his head.

'I don't know,' Thaddeus said. 'We'd better take a look.' He got out of his armchair. 'Go and check the prisoners,' he ordered the Pigeon-Poo Gang. He felt a growing sense of alarm. Something was wrong. He knew it.

The pigeons flew away along the corridor. A loud cooing told Thaddeus all he needed to know. 'They've escaped!' the leader of the gang confirmed when he returned.

'But how?' Thaddeus E. Fox cursed his ill luck.

'Zey couldn't have got out wizout 'elp,' Kebab Claude said.

'But no one's been here this afternoon,' Thaddeus fumed. 'Except those zombie chickens.'

'What zombie chickens?' Tiny Tony Tiddles demanded.

'The three that came to check if Rooster had been eating garlic,' Thaddeus dismissed the question. 'The countess sent them.'

'It was daylight,' Tiny Tony Tiddles said slowly. 'The countess was asleep.'

Thaddeus stared at him. Tiddles was right. The countess couldn't have sent them.

'Three chickens, did you say?' asked Kebab Claude. 'What were zey like?'

'Pretty hideous . . .' Thaddeus E. Fox tried to remember. 'One was small with a fat tummy. One had feathery boots . . .' He stopped. His voice trailed off.

'Let me guess,' Tiny Tony Tiddles said. 'The other one had specs.' He gave a shake of his head. 'Those weren't chicken zombies, dude. Those were

174

Professor Rooster's elite chicken squad in disguise.'

'I thought you said zey were dumb,' Claude said, puzzled. 'Sounds like zey're pretty smart to me.'

Thaddeus E. Fox gave a roar of rage. He smashed his cane on the floor. He rushed into the kitchen and ripped all the stuffing out of the armchair and shredded it. The chickens! They had tricked him again! Well, if they wanted to play dirty then so would he. Pretending the armchair stuffing was Amy, Boo and Ruth, he tossed it into the air with his teeth and watched it flutter down into the fireplace and catch light.

'Gentlemen,' he hissed, 'change of plan. We won't wait for nightfall. We'll raid the chicken sheds now.'

'I wish they'd hurry up!' Amy, Boo and Ruth struggled across the moor with the granny chickens. The grannies kept stopping to admire the view and complain about their corns. 'We'll never make it at this rate!'

Just then they heard angry barking coming from the direction of the hall.

'It's Fox!' Boo whispered.

'He must have realised he's been tricked,' Ruth gulped.

The barking came again.

'You two go on ahead and warn the professor!' Amy urged.

'Are you sure, Amy?' Ruth asked.

'Yes.' The barking was getting louder. 'I'll get the grannies under cover. It's the chickens in the sheds Fox is after. He won't bother with a lot of scrawny old granny hens.'

'But . . .' Boo hesitated.

'Go!' Amy insisted. 'Take Ichabod with you,' she added.

Ichabod Comb was looking a lot better. He was still pretty much featherless, but at least the goo had gone. He might be able to help.

'Okay!' Boo and Ruth scuttled off with the rooster.

'Time for a rest!' Amy squawked at the grannies. 'Over here.' Amy led them away from the path out

onto the moor where the grass was thick and tufty. 'This will do!' She picked a spot dense with clumps of heather. The grannies flopped onto the springy plants. Amy watched, satisfied. The hens were hard to spot amongst the heather unless you were looking for them. And Thaddeus wouldn't waste time with that. She decided to leave them here until the fight was over. It was probably the safest place.

'Anyone feeling peckish?' Granny Wishbone fished under her wing and produced a net bag full of grain.

'Yes, I am,' said Amy. She was starving. Breakfast seemed a very long time ago.

Granny Wishbone opened the bag carefully. She gave Amy the tiniest morsel of grain she could find and set about gobbling up the rest.

'Thanks a lot,' said Amy.

PHUT!

She looked up. Three grey and purple birds circled overhead. 'The Pigeon-Poo Gang!' she gasped. They had sniffed out the grain! 'Quick!' she cried. 'Hide the grain!'

Granny Wishbone kept scoffing.

PHUT! PHUT! PHUT!

The pigeons began an aerial bombardment. The hens scuttled this way and that.

'Put it away!' Amy screamed. 'Before they sludge us to death.'

PHUT! PHUT! PHUT!

The Pigeon-Poo Gang flew back in the opposite direction.

'I can't!' Granny Wishbone had been hit. Her beak was glued to her corns.

'Get under cover!' shouted Amy.

The grannies wriggled under the heather.

Amy looked about for a weapon. She spied Granny Wishbone's Zimmer frame. 'Can I borrow this for a second?' she said.

'No!' Granny Wishbone screeched. 'That's my best one.'

'Too bad.' Amy grabbed the Zimmer frame. The pigeons circled again. 'Now for a new world record throw!' Amy took aim and hurled the Zimmer frame into the air.

BASH! It hit the three pigeons bang on the beaks. They plummeted towards the ground, then flew off haphazardly across the moor in the direction of the Deep Dark Woods.

'Ha, ha!' Amy crowed. 'Not bad for a beginner. Wait there,' she told the grannies, 'I'll be back soon.' She scuttled off across the moor towards Fogsham Farm.

Chapter Eighteen

Amy hopped over the farmyard wall and sneaked towards the sleeping coop. Thaddeus E. Fox and his friends hadn't reached the farm yet. They must still be figuring out what had happened to the countess.

'Pssssst! Amy!' Boo's voice came from the hospital shed. 'Over here!'

Amy scuttled over. The door opened a fraction. Amy squeezed through.

Boo and Ruth were there. So were the professor and James Pond. James Pond looked better than he had in the dungeon but Amy could tell from his haunted expression that he was still spooked. Amy wasn't sure how much help he would be. It was down to Professor Rooster and his elite chicken squad to defend the roost.

Amy gave them her news about the grannies.

'So we don't need to worry about the Pigeon-Poo Gang,' Professor Rooster concluded. 'Well done, Amy.'

'Thanks!' Amy felt shy again. It was cool getting praise from the professor but she didn't know what to say in reply. 'Where's everyone else?' she asked instead.

'In the underground bunker,' Professor Rooster said.

'What underground bunker?'

'Rossiter and his chickens have converted Thaddeus's tunnel into a hidey-hole,' Professor Rooster explained. 'We've blocked the entrance beside the wall with cow dung. There's no way Fox and his pals will want to get that on their fur. The only way into the bunker is through here.'

'What about the juice shed? Didn't he dig a tunnel into that as well?' Amy asked.

'Ichabod nailed the floor down so tight a woodlouse couldn't get through it,' James Pond said.

Amy nodded. 'What weapons have we got?' she asked.

'Not many, I'm afraid,' said Professor Rooster. 'I only put standard vampire issue in the Emergency Chicken Pack and you've used quite a lot of that already. There's the hammer, the pencil, the

sharpener, the grease squirt and the magnifying glass. Then there's the mite blaster, of course. And we found some string, which might come in useful. And an old bucket.'

Some string and an old bucket! Amy tried to figure out how they would help.

KNOCK! KNOCK! KNOCK!

The chickens jumped.

'I know you're in there, Rooster,' Thaddeus's voice came through the planks. 'We can do this the easy way or the hard way. You and your chickens surrender and we won't harm the others. If you don't, we'll kill the lot of you.'

'No deal, Fox,' Professor Rooster shouted back. 'We chickens stick together.' He smiled at Amy. She felt her heart glow with pride.

'All right,' Thaddeus snarled. 'Don't say you weren't warned.'

Amy heard muttering.

BOOMPH! The door of the shed rattled.

Ruth fixed the tube into the mite blaster. 'We've only got one tube,' she said. 'We mustn't waste it.'

182

The door rattled again. 'Put your back into it, Claude!' Thaddeus shouted.

Amy peeped through the window of the chicken shed. Kebab Claude was backing up, ready for another charge at the door.

'I wish he'd fall over!' Boo was beside her.

'What did you say?' Amy pulled a bit of straw out of her ears. It had been lurking in there all the time.

'I said I wish he'd fall over,' Boo repeated.

An idea pinged into Amy's head replacing the straw.

'He will if I squirt grease at him.' She picked up the canister.

'That's a good idea, Amy,' Professor Rooster said slowly. 'Then we can keep the mite blaster up our wings for later.' He scratched his crop. 'The question is how are you going to stop Kebab Claude without the villains seeing you?'

Amy considered for a minute. 'I know!' She'd had another good idea. Getting rid of that straw between her ears had made all the difference. 'I'll hide under the bucket!'

 183

BOOMPH! Kebab Claude thudded into the front door. Two of the nails fell out. James Pond hammered them back in. 'We need to hurry,' he said. 'The planks are giving way.'

'Very well,' Professor Rooster said. 'Let's put Amy's plan into action.'

Amy did some breathing exercises while Ruth made two spy holes in the bucket with a nail and a third one at about tummy height for Amy to stick the grease squirt nozzle through. Amy tried the nozzle for size.

'Perfect!' Ruth said.

'All clear!' Boo was keeping watch at the window. 'The villains are still at the front.'

Ruth levered open a plank at the back of the shed with the claw of the hammer. Amy crept out. Ruth handed Amy the grease squirt and lifted the bucket over her head.

Everything went dark.

'Are you all right in there?' Ruth hissed.

'Yes, fine.' Amy's voice echoed around the bucket.

'Good luck!' Professor Rooster said.

Amy heard the *BANG BANG BANG* of nails being driven back through the planks. She was on her own: for now, anyway.

Amy tiptoed round the corner of the shed and stopped. She sank to her knees so that the rim of the bucket was on the ground, completely covering her legs. She didn't want the villains to see the bucket moving or they would guess that something chickeny was going on. She would have to take it in stages.

She peeped out of the spy holes.

There was Thaddeus E. Fox, immaculate in his top hat and tails. Tiny Tony Tiddles paced impatiently beside him with his fedora at a jaunty angle. She would have to be careful of the cat, Amy decided. He looked tricky. She got to her feet and tottered off again.

TRIP! Amy felt her left foot catch on something. She staggered forwards, the bucket swivelling about on her head. Somehow she managed to keep her balance. She stopped again and peeped through the spy holes in the direction she had come. A green rubber tube zigzagged along the ground. At first she thought it might be a grass snake but then she realised she had tripped over the hosepipe.

'Go further back!' Thaddeus ordered. 'Get some speed up this time.'

Amy turned her attention back to the villains. Kebab Claude had retreated to the farmyard wall. Thaddeus and Tiny Tony had their eyes on him. She scuttled forward.

SPLODGE!

A nasty smell rose from the ground. Amy glanced

down. Her feet were all brown. *Honestly!* Now she'd trodden in a cowpat!

She took a few more steps and poked the grease squirt nozzle through the tummy hole.

KALUMP! KALUMP! KALUMP! KALUMP! KALUMP!

Kebab Claude thundered towards the shed.

Amy's wing closed on the grease squirt button. *Any minute now,* she thought. Kebab Claude's paws came into view. Amy squeezed the button as hard as she could.

FTSSSSSSSSSSSSS! The grease squirted out of the nozzle and onto Kebab Claude.

'Whoaaaooooaaaoooo!' Kebab Claude scrabbled for a hold with his claws.

'What's the matter?' Thaddeus shouted at him.

FTSSSSSSSSSSSSS! Amy squeezed again.

'I slipped on ze ice!'

From her vantage point in the bucket Amy saw Kebab Claude's paws circle in front of her as if he was doing the doggy paddle. Her heart thumped. Kebab was getting dangerously close to knocking the bucket

over. But if she tried to escape now, the villains would see it moving. She would have to wait.

'Ice?' Thaddeus echoed. 'There wasn't any ice there a minute ago.'

CRASH! Kebab Claude couldn't stay upright any more. He crashed to the ground and skidded towards Amy.

SMASH! He smashed into the bucket.

Amy felt herself being catapulted into the air. The bucket flew off. She landed in a heap in the cowpat, still clutching the grease squirt.

Amy looked up. Three pairs of yellow eyes glared down at her. 'Er . . . hello,' she said.

'You again!' Thaddeus E. Fox snarled.

'Run, Amy!'

Amy looked up. Boo stood a little way away from her. She was holding the end of the hosepipe in her wings. Behind her, by the hospital shed, was Ruth.

FTSSSSSSSSSSSSSSS! 'Take that, losers!' Amy gave one final push on the grease squirt button and ran for her life back towards the hospital shed.

'Get her!' The fox, the dog and the cat set off in

pursuit of Amy. 'Owwwwwwwww!'

Amy glanced behind. The grease squirt had done its job again. The three baddies fell over in the cowpat.

'This is disgusting!' howled Kebab Claude.

'It's your fault, Fox!' yowled Tiny Tony Tiddles.

'Shut up!' Thaddeus E. Fox lashed out at them both. His glossy red fur was covered in muck. It was in his tail. It was in his whiskers. It was up his nose. Somehow or other it had even got in his ears. How he hated those chickens!

Amy reached Boo. 'Time those villains had a bath!' Boo said.

Amy helped her friend grip the end of the hosepipe.

'Turn the water on, Ruth!' Boo shouted.

Ruth turned on the tap.

SPLOOSH!

A jet of water shot out of the end of the hosepipe and hit Thaddeus in the face. It streamed off him onto the other two animals in an imitation of a waterfall, and dripped onto the gloopy remains of the cowpat.

'I hate water!' Tiny Tony Tiddles screamed.

The three villains paddled and flopped and wallowed.

'Time for a dose of mites!' Ruth stepped forward with the mite blaster.

'No!' the villains begged.

'All right, then,' Ruth relented. 'But go. Right now, or I'll blast you.'

'Yeah, time to push off!' Amy yelled.

The villains struggled to their feet. Tiny Tony Tiddles stalked away and disappeared onto the moor. Kebab Claude limped after him.

Thaddeus E. Fox had reached the farmyard wall. He paused with one paw in the air and looked back.

'You heard!' Professor Rooster stood beside his elite chicken squad. He had the string in one wing. The other he placed on Amy's shoulder. 'Push off! Or we'll tie you up and leave you for the farmer.'

'I'll get you for this, Rooster!' Thaddeus snarled. 'If it's the last thing I do.' He jumped over the wall and was gone.

'Hooray!' Amy cried. 'We did it!' She gave Boo and Ruth a huge hug. Then she turned to the professor. She still had something she needed to get off her chest. 'I'm sorry I didn't tell you about James Pond, Professor,' she blurted out. 'It was my idea to ask him to help. I thought it wouldn't matter if you didn't find out, but I can see now that it did.'

'It's all right, Amy,' Professor Rooster said gently. 'I was partly to blame for giving you such a difficult mission in the first place. The important thing is you did it in the end.' He fixed Amy with a stern look. 'But next time, tell me the truth, okay?'

'Okay!' Amy wanted to punch the air with joy. The professor had forgiven her. She promised herself she wouldn't do anything silly like that again. EVER.

'Congratulations to you all!' Professor Rooster smiled at his team. 'Chicken Mission accomplished.'

Epilogue

Ichabod Comb sat at the bar in the juice shed. Since the defeat of Stella von Fangula and inspired by the false name the villains had adopted for Bloodsucker Hall, the shed had been renamed by the chickens of Fogsham Farm as The Happy Hen, which was altogether a far nicer name than the one it had before, Ichabod agreed. He helped himself to a worm juice and a packet of grub scratchings with a satisfied sigh. It wasn't only that the curse had been lifted: the granny hens had gone home to their smallholding at last. He had thought they would never stop partying.

'All right, Ichabod?' Rossiter Brown came and sat down beside him. 'Feeling better?'

'Much better, thanks,' Ichabod Comb said. The pain in his leg had gone and his wings had returned to full feather. He could hardly remember being a zombie at all, except that it had been rather gooey.

'I brought you this.' Rossiter Brown placed a

newspaper on the bar. Ichabod Comb scanned the front page.

'Thanks,' said Ichabod.

THE DAILY SNAIL

50p

Curse of Fogsham Farm Lifted!
Rooster and his team defeat
Fox and the MOST WANTED Gang!
Amy Cluckbucket smashes World
Zimmer Frame Throwing Record.

There was silence for a minute.

'No one blames you for what happened at Bloodsucker Hall, Ichabod,' Rossiter Brown said eventually. 'It was an easy mistake to make.'

Ichabod felt awkward. It was the first time since the events of recent days that anyone had actually brought up with him how the Countess Stella von

Fangula had awoken from her grave. He gave a little nod.

'I just wanted you to know.' Rossiter Brown got up to go.

Ichabod Comb waited until the rooster had left the juice shed. It was decent of Rossiter Brown to say that, he decided. And it made him feel much better about things. He vaguely remembered visiting Bloodsucker Hall. And he had been wondering if the whole von Fangula problem had been somehow his responsibility although he couldn't quite remember how: being a zombie seemed to have zapped his brain. Still, it was a relief to know none of the other chickens in the coop held it against him. He could forget all about it now.

Ichabod Comb felt a renewed sense of adventure. It was time he went on another expedition. In fact, he would go as soon as the spring came! He hopped off his stool and fetched a little book from behind the bar. The grannies had left it behind by mistake. It was a guidebook of the moor.

He turned the pages. There were all sorts of exciting

things to do nearby. He picked out his three favourites and wrote them laboriously on a piece of paper.

Sprognockle Spooky Ghost Walk
Haunted Catacombs of Doom Church
Witch's Cauldron at Wartspell Crags

Ichabod Comb tore the paper into three, folded each piece up and put them in a cup. Then he closed his eyes and picked one out with his wing and unfolded it again.

Witch's Cauldron at Wartspell Crags

That would do very nicely. He'd always wanted to go to Wartspell Crags. He began to plan the trip in his head.

After all, thought Ichabod Comb, *what could possibly go wrong this time?*

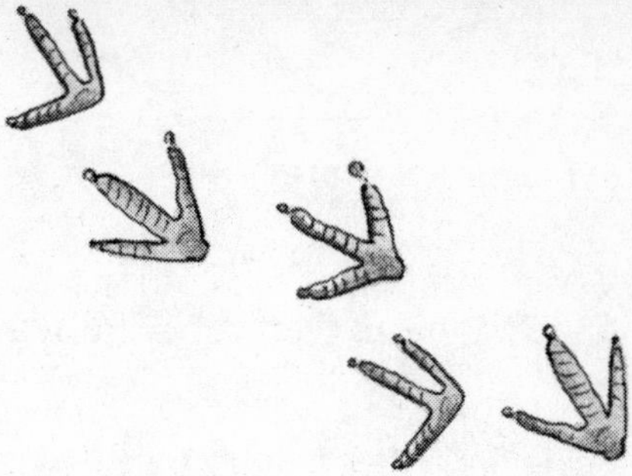

Find out what other
missions the
Elite Chicken Squad
have cracked . . .

JENNIFER GRAY

WINNER Red House Children's Book Award

Chicken Mission

Danger in the
Deep Dark Woods

Don't miss . . .

Out Now!

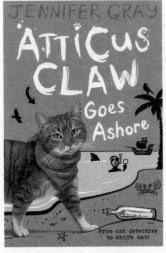